FATED TO WOLVES

POWER MAGIC
BOOK ONE

AMELIA SHAW

TAMSIN BAKER

Owning a gym and being a five-foot-six-inch-tall woman who weighed over two hundred pounds was always going to raise eyebrows. The fact that I was also a witch... well, that would have set tongues wagging if they knew.

It was a real shame that us supernaturals were banned from exposing ourselves to the human population. My gym was fifty/fifty supernaturals and humans, and I would have loved for some of the humans who sneered down their noses at me to know that I could easily turn them into fat, ugly toads.

I would have been doing the world a favor and making their outsides match their insides.

"Hey Tania," George called out as he swiped his membership card at the front desk.

"Hi George," I greeted a long-time member walking in to train, then frowned at the black eye he was sporting. "What happened there?"

He shrugged his massive shoulders. "I was having a drink

with my girl on Saturday night, just chatting and having a good time..."

I groaned. "And some asshole picked you out for a fight?"

Like most of my clients, George was a power lifter. He was huge. Six foot two and about three hundred and fifty pounds.

He grinned at me. "You know I never start those fights."

I couldn't help the laugh that bubbled up out of nowhere. "Yeah, but you always finish them."

He chuckled and headed off into the main section of the gym. The music changed the moment he stepped into the room. George's choice today, like always, was Ramstein, the heavy metal bass and German lyrics bouncing around the walls of my gym.

I turned to yell out at him. "George!"

His laughter was the only response, and I heaved a pretend-dramatic sigh. George wasn't just a friend and a long-standing patron. He was also a warlock, and liked to play DJ with my sound system when he was here at the gym.

I didn't bother making a correction. The music he chose suited the lifting he did, and that inspired most of the guys around him. It was good for morale, and I didn't mind Ramstein. Not at all. But I liked to pretend it annoyed me.

The door opened and a blonde chick flounced in, her bare midriff and long ponytail making me instantly prickle. This wasn't the sort of gym that did aerobics classes.

"Hello," I greeted her with a practiced smile. "I'm Tania, the owner. Can I help you?"

If I'd been tempted to admonish myself for judging her too quickly, her next words silenced my inner judge completely.

"*You* own this place?" she asked, her gaze raking over my body with a downturn of her lips.

I flicked my long brown hair back over my shoulders and straightened my spine. "Have done for over ten years now. Most of my clients here are power lifters and compete in strong-man or strong-woman competitions. Although you're welcome to train at any capacity, we don't offer classes, boxing or aerobics."

The woman struck a pose, crossing her arms over her chest. "I was told you did."

Stay calm.

I forced myself to take a breath and keep the smile plastered on my face. "You're probably looking for the women's-only gym down the block. A hundred feet that way," I pointed to my right. "You can't miss it. It's *pink.*"

The woman's eyes flared with a hatred I'd put up with since I was a teenager. Good-looking popular girls didn't like big girls like me.

Especially ones that put them in their place.

"Thanks." She pivoted on the balls of her feet and flounced right out again.

The cackling sound that came in the door following the blonde's departure signaled that my best friend, Jaydy, had arrived. She was a power lifter and sometime-trainer here at the gym. She was also a powerful witch.

We had known each other through school and the friendship had only strengthened since then.

"How long did it take you to get rid of her?" Jaydy asked as she stepped in the door, work-out bag slung over her right shoulder.

I shrugged. "Don't know. Sixty seconds, maybe?"

Her smile was contagious. "You're getting faster."

"And you're late," I told her, glancing up at the clock. "Dani's been here for ages."

She swiped her card and hurried through the door. "Shit. Thanks!"

I turned to watch as she rushed off to meet with Dani, a client who'd started her routine without Jaydy.

They exchanged some words, including what I had to assume was an apology from Jaydy for being late. I couldn't hear a thing with George's chosen music pumping over the speakers.

I chuckled to myself and got back to work. By the time my shift was done, I was exhausted. But that didn't mean I wasn't going to train.

George was packing up and Jaydy was long gone.

"You know I can stay. Spot you?" George said, zipping up his bag. His face dripped with sweat. He'd been here three hours already.

"Nah. You know I'm all good." I waggled my eyebrows at him. My magic wouldn't allow me to get hurt, and he knew it. "See you tomorrow?"

He nodded. "Yeah. Competition's in four weeks. No time to slack off now."

I waved goodnight to him, followed him to the entrance and locked the front door. One thing I'd never gotten truly comfortable with, was letting people watch me train.

Or compete.

Despite ten years of training, wishing, and dreaming, I was yet to follow through with my first competition. It was foolish, I knew. But every time I got close, something stopped me.

Fear of failure, perhaps? Of being seen for who I truly was?

I didn't really know, but I'd given up trying to understand. And my friends had given up trying to talk me into competing.

I got into my training session, loving the burn in my muscles as I pushed through the weights. My heart pounded and sweat ran down my face.

When I was most of the way through the session, the pain began to ease, and then stopped. A wave of ecstasy flowed over me. The endorphins kicking in, big time.

Better than drugs. Better than sex.

Especially considering my limited experience with both.

I finished the session on a natural high, then cleaned up and put all my weights away. My legs were shaking from the stress of finishing some killer squats, but luckily I didn't live far from the gym. In fact, I lived above it. I could practically hear my shower upstairs calling me from where I stood.

I trudged to my office, a small room at the back of the huge warehouse that held a desk, an old computer, and contained the spiral stairwell that led up to my apartment on the next level.

I'd worked hard to build this business when I first started and bought the building a few years ago, converting the rooms on top of the gym into a cozy home for myself.

My right foot had just hit the first step of the spiral staircase when I heard a loud knocking at the front entrance.

I frowned at the sound. This was an industrial area. I rarely saw anyone on the streets past six p.m. Except those going to one of the two gyms. Mine and the fluffy pink one.

Mine was clearly closed.

I decided to ignore the knocking and took another step up the stairs, only to have the sound intensify.

Bang, bang, bang, bang, bang.

Whoever it was, didn't want to take no for an answer. I groaned loudly and rolled my eyes. But I couldn't ignore the urgency evident in the sound.

I was sweaty and hungry and very quickly becoming hangry. I stomped to the front door, preparing to blast whoever it was with a few choice words. I flicked on the main lights as I went. Between my magic and my boxing skills I could handle most threats that came to my door. But it still helped to be able to see who I may need to fight.

When the final light flicked on, the person standing on the

other side of my front entrance was the last person I expected to see. "Harry?"

I rushed to open the door. My friend was in trouble. Blood covered his white shirt and dripped onto the concrete sidewalk beneath his feet.

As soon as the door opened, I threw up a protection spell that would allow Harry to come inside but stop anyone else from entering. "What happened?"

I reached out for him, desperate to help. Harry took one step toward me before collapsing into my arms.

"Oof." He was heavier than I expected, and I would have dropped him if I hadn't bolstered my strength with my magic. I grabbed onto his sagging body and managed to drag him fully inside and sit down on my white-tiled foyer floor with his head in my lap.

I stroked his short dark hair and whispered. "Who did this to you?"

He stared up at me, his brown eyes filled with shame. "It was me. A spell... it backfired."

Hot tears filled my eyes and leaked down my cheeks when I saw how much blood was pooling around us. "No Harry... I'll fix you."

I put out my hand, my arm trembling with the stress of seeing my childhood friend bleeding out before my eyes. I began to chant, a basic healing spell. I'd never mastered more than high school level magic when it came to healing, and I wasn't sure what I was going to be able to do to help him, but I had to try.

My parents had normal jobs. There were a limited number of magical jobs within our world, and they'd encouraged me to live outside the warlock realm where I'd been raised. I'd crossed over with them into the human world straight after high school, and as a result, my magic wasn't as well-developed as it could have been.

White light sparked from my fingers and passed over Harry as more tears leaked down my face. But nothing changed in relation to his injuries.

"Come on!" I ground out, forcing more magic into the spell.

Harry reached for my arm, his wet fingers leaving sticky, bloody fingerprints on my skin. "It's okay... Tan. It's okay."

"Why didn't you go to your parents?" I demanded of him, anger born of fear ripping into me. I couldn't lose him. He was one of my oldest friends. "They could have fixed you. Helped you."

He chuckled softly, then coughed, sending more blood over his lips and down his chin. "They don't deserve the last of my magic."

"What do you mean?" I asked him.

"The spell... that's killing me. It's a genie spell."

I gasped. Surely, he hadn't been trying to do a forbidden spell? "No! You didn't..."

He groaned, his eyes closing. "You know I only ever wanted one thing."

"For your parents to accept you... for who you really are," I whispered, hoisting him higher so I could cradle him in my arms.

Harry was gay, a fact that had been obvious since he was little. His parents had rejected any notion of him not being 'normal' and he'd spent most of his teenage years living at my house.

My parents had loved him like a son. And to me, an only child, he'd been the closest thing to a brother I'd ever had. Even if we'd drifted apart over the last ten years, I still loved him with all my heart.

I shook him a little. "Harry, I would have helped you if I'd known you were struggling this much. You could have lived here with me. We could have been the odd couple all over again."

He sighed, long and heavy. "I should have come here earlier.

But I should have done a lot of things. Now stop and listen to me. What is your greatest wish, Tan?"

"For you to live!" I cried, a sob catching in my throat as Harry's eyes began to close, his skin as pale as the white tiles beneath us.

"No." His voice was a choked whisper. "You always said you wished your magic matched your physical strength. Do you still wish that?"

"You remember that?" I said, and he nodded.

As two outcasts at a magical high school we'd often wished for things to be different. Part of me had wanted to be small and sexy, but most of me was proud of my curves and strength. When that size hadn't translated into anything special magically, I'd often wished for more.

I gulped. "Yes, of course I do. But not just for me. For all the big girls out there. That our strength, our power, our size... meant something more than just being... fat."

Harry forced his eyes open, a strange green mist floating across them. His lips trembled as he lifted his blood-covered hand and touched my cheek.

Then he said one final word, "Granted."

His touch turned hot, tingling against my flesh. I gasped at the sensation, then the feeling was gone, and so was Harry.

His head fell back and I didn't worry about being composed any longer. I pulled his head to my chest and sobbed my heart out. "Oh, Harry, I'm sorry. I'm so so sorry. Please Harry. Come back..."

TWO

The next week passed in a blur of pain. The magical council ruled Harry's death a suicide, which meant he was buried quickly, and with a private funeral service.

It was meant to be family only, but my parents and I muscled our way in. Harry's parents seemed grateful for the company in the graveyard, though afterwards they didn't even thank us for attending.

Their son had just died, so part of me understood why they were seemingly so rude. But considering my parents were owed thanks for practically raising their son when they wouldn't, part of me couldn't stop being angry at them.

I spent the week with my parents, in their country house an hour out of town. After I'd called the paramedics and they arrived and took away Harry's body, I'd spent ages scrubbing the white tiles in my foyer to get rid of Harry's blood. Then I had lay down in the same exact spot and cried for so long the sun had come up and the first of my staff arrived to start their shifts.

Luckily for me, I had great employees. Daniella had scooped

me up and forced me back to my apartment for a shower, then told me to take the week off and she'd handle everything.

I checked in once or twice and she did seem to have everything under control. George had sent his condolences and followed up with a report about how the gym was faring. My business was surviving without me, but it was time to go back. I packed my bags and headed out to my parents' living room.

My mom was there, in her apron and sneakers. "Hey, sweetie. I made breakfast. Come eat."

By 'made breakfast', she meant she'd waved her hands around and conjured up the most magnificent feast imaginable. "Wow Mom, it looks great."

My mom, unlike me, was a petite little thing with a good deal of magic. I'd gotten my size from my father, who'd played NFL as an enforcer. Even at sixty, he was still fit, and just as big as ever.

Speak of the devil.

"How's my girl this morning?" Dad asked, walking into the room and putting his arm around my shoulders. "You know you don't need to go back to the city so soon. Despite the reason you came home, we've loved having you here."

I hugged him back, then sat down at the breakfast table to start eating. My mom was used to cooking for my father, who happened to have a voracious appetite, and that meant the food was freaking delicious and there was always more than enough.

Just for breakfast, I had the choice of bacon and eggs, sausage and tomatoes, waffles and fruit, porridge and buttered toast. And if I didn't have some of everything, my mom would have had plenty to say about that.

"I'd love to stay," I told them truthfully, reaching for the platter of bacon and eggs. "I've put on five pounds since I got here."

Not that I cared. What was another five pounds?

My father chuckled. "You've gotten too thin. You're training too hard."

I rolled my eyes. "Too thin, Dad? That's a first."

"Maybe we should get an apartment in the city too," Mom suggested. "I could bring you food. Make sure you're looking after yourself."

I would have laughed, assuming they were joking, but when I glanced up from my breakfast to look at Mom, then my dad, I could tell they really were worried about me. "If you guys want to get an apartment in the city, I'd love to have you around more, but don't just do it for my sake."

Mom glanced over at Dad. "Your father misses training."

Dad coughed loudly, "Oh, well..."

Mom gave him a sweet smile. "It's okay, sweetheart. I know the quiet life here in the country wasn't your choice; it was mine."

Oh my God. They were serious.

I looked at my dad. "There's a strongman comp in four weeks, Dad. Maybe you could enter and compete?"

Dad grabbed for the waffles. "Oh, no. I'm way past competitions."

I glanced at Mom who was nodding softly, encouraging me to continue.

I turned back to him. "If you're serious about spending more time in the city, I'd love some help at the gym, Dad. I do the best I can, but I know the men especially would benefit from a guy like you around to help."

It had actually been on my mind recently, that I didn't have anyone to help my elites.

"George, for example," I said. "He needs help with technique, and to be honest I think his diet needs work. He's about ten kilos less than he should be, but I don't feel qualified to advise him."

Dad munched on his waffles, scooping food into his mouth at an impressive rate. "That's nice of you to say, Tania, but—"

"Oh, if you don't want to do it, that's totally fine," I said, reaching for the juice. "I know you're busy."

Cleaning your car... gardening...

There must have been something in my tone, because Dad narrowed his eyes. Mom whipped out a real estate brochure. "I was looking at this place. It needs a lot of work, but there's something special about it."

I pulled the advertisement closer, staring down at a house I'd walked past a hundred times. It was between the gym and my local grocery store. "Mom, this place is practically a pull-down-and-rebuild job."

It was a mansion, about three blocks from my gym. But it'd been abandoned for decades, or certainly looked like it. I had noticed it both because of its impressive size, but also the sorry state it was in.

She shrugged, eating her fruit and porridge. "I need a project. I'm a bit bored, to be honest."

I frowned at her, not sure she'd really thought this through. "You know you can't just snap your fingers and renovate the whole place with magic, Mom?"

Unlike me, my mother's magic was fantastic. She was more powerful than both my father and I put together.

She rolled her eyes in a mocking type of way. "I know, Tania. I've lived in the human world for a long time. I know what I can get away with and what I can't."

I looked from my mother, to my father, and back again. "If you two are serious, I'd love to have you close. I've missed you."

It seemed like such a simple thing to say, but the feelings that descended were hot and heavy. I swallowed hard, trying not to cry. Maybe I'd missed them more than I wanted to admit. And this week, dealing with Harry's death, I felt like I needed them a little more than usual.

"Good," Mom said, calm as ever. "Because I put an offer on it last week."

Dad's jaw dropped. "You *what*?"

I began to laugh. They hadn't changed. "So... when do you move in?"

She shrugged. "The agent said we can move in anytime. The money's just sitting in the account, so as soon as you're ready, Magnus?"

I looked over at Dad, whose huge physical presence made the fact that his wife ran rings around him, even funnier. "What do you say, Dad?"

He grabbed for the bread basket. "Why not? I always wanted to live in a creepy old mansion."

I chuckled, shaking my head. My parents were awesome and probably added to my long list of why I didn't have a husband yet. Their relationship was so perfect, and my standards were high.

I left after breakfast and drove the hour back to the city. The fact that my parents would soon follow gave me more comfort than I wanted to admit.

It was Saturday, so traffic was minimal. I got home faster than I first planned. I drove into my designated car spot and turned off the engine. Then I couldn't get out. I just sat there, my arms and legs refusing to move.

Every time I closed my eyes, I saw Harry. Dying. Bleeding all over himself. And me. My white floor covered with thick, dark pools of crimson death.

I knew I couldn't sit out here forever. Eventually I gathered the courage and forced myself to move. Still, my hand shook as I reached for the handle and pushed open my door. I could do this. I could.

"Tania!" Jaydy's voice rang out across the carpark.

I turned to greet my bestie. "Hey Jaydy." I managed a smile. "How are you?"

"How are *you* is a more relevant question?" She rushed up to hug me.

I tried not to crumble into her hug, and instead held myself stiff. "I'm okay. You know."

She pulled back and stared into my eyes. "Yeah, I do. Harry was like a brother to you."

I swallowed hard against the lump in my throat and managed to say, "Yeah, he was."

I pocketed my car keys and walked toward the front door of my gym, grateful for Jaydy's company. "How's everything been in my absence?"

She grinned at me. "Fine. Though George has been telling everyone he's in charge now."

I had to laugh at that one, though chuckling felt weird and foreign in my still-grieving body. "Yeah… I can imagine."

We reached the glass front entrance and I stopped.

Jaydy stepped around me and opened the door for me. "You really okay, hon?"

I inhaled sharply, my breath catching in my throat. "To be honest, I don't know."

My friend linked her arm in mine. "The first time is always going to be the worst. Wanna walk in together?"

I nodded, my heart pounding. "Yeah, thanks."

That first step was definitely the hardest. My legs shook but I surged forward into my gym. My home.

The floor was clean. No blood whatsoever. In fact, the white tiles were pristine.

Daniella was manning the desk and when she saw me, she smiled brightly. "Welcome back."

I waved at her, then pulled Jaydy's arm to walk around the spot where Harry had died. I didn't want to step foot there. Ever again.

As we passed the place where Harry had told me my wish was granted, a thought occurred to me.

"Hey Jaydy. Have you done any magic lately?" She was one of the strongest women I knew. She trained for hours, daily, and usually won her weight division at comps.

She shrugged. "Just my normal stuff. Nothing special. Why?"

"No reason," I said, shaking my head. Surely Harry hadn't been serious about achieving the genie spell? It was impossible. A myth. Something we had all laughed about as kids.

But one thing was certain. He'd messed with some serious magic that he shouldn't have. And it had killed him.

The gym was relatively quiet for a Saturday morning, so after checking in with Daniella and making sure there were no issues I needed to deal with, I excused myself and went upstairs.

Everything was where I'd left it, yet something felt odd. Maybe it was just me? I was different somehow and it wasn't simply grief from Harry's passing. I couldn't quite pinpoint what it was, though.

I sighed and went into my bedroom to unpack my clothes. Mom had washed everything for me, magically, so I was coming home with a suitcase full of clean clothes.

I couldn't help chuckling as I put everything away. She had even made them smell like roses, as if they'd been lovingly hand-washed.

Then it was time to clean out the refrigerator, and sit down. Everything inside me ached, right down to my bones. I hadn't trained all week, but I couldn't face going down there now. Not with more and more people arriving by the hour.

Maybe tonight.

Or tomorrow.

George was sure to come find me the next time he came in, but for the moment, my heart needed a rest. I pulled back the covers on my queen-sized bed and climbed in, still clothed.

Later, I'd be strong enough to deal with my business, and the fact that my parents were moving to town.

For now, I needed to grieve the loss of the man I'd considered my brother.

I still couldn't believe he'd died for such a stupid reason. The genie wish was a myth, and clearly not something that was real. My poor dear Harry had died, for nothing.

THREE

TANIA

I deliberately avoided people over the next few days. I worked behind the scenes, in the office, or did the close of day or the start when it was usually quieter, not wanting to have to deal with the strain of putting on a fake positive front for my gym customers and staff.

My body ached from the lack of training, and my heart hurt for the loss of my childhood friend. My brother.

On Wednesday night, after everyone had left, I decided it was time to get back into my work outs. Nothing made me feel better, nor lifted the depression off me, like exercise. And Harry would have hated to see me moping around.

I set up my weights and got to work, pushing myself further than I normally would. Despite the fact I'd had a week off, and still wasn't feeling like myself, the work out was easy. Too easy.

I checked the weights but I hadn't made any errors.

Strange.

I pushed to the end of the session, my heart pounding and

sweat rolling down my face. I'd put on weight the past week; I could feel it within my body already. Not that I cared about my size, but it was the loss of muscle that I wasn't happy about.

When I was finished, I cleaned up and put everything away.

I was exhausted, so instead of doing my normal 'human style' lock up, I flicked my hand toward the front door, aiming to lock it using my magic. I wasn't sure my powers would extend that far, but I figured it couldn't hurt to try.

The door locked, with a loud click, the curtains rolled down, and the lights in the front half of the warehouse flicked off.

My jaw dropped. Sure, that was what I'd planned to do next, but there was no way I'd have thought I could do it with just my magic.

I stood up, and with a shaking hand, waved my fingers over a dumb bell I'd left at my feet, telling it to go back to its place on the rack.

I watched in awe as the weight flew up to where it should go and nestled in neatly with the other weights.

"Holy shit."

It wasn't possible. No way. I'd never had this sort of power before—magical or physical.

I had to test it out properly. I finished turning off all the lights in the normal, human way, and went up to my apartment for a shower. I washed my hair and took my time scrubbing the sweat from my skin, my mind awhirl with possibilities.

The genie spell that had killed Harry was powerful. But even so, surely the spell wouldn't really have given Harry the power to impart a single wish?

If it had, and if Harry really had blessed me with the same amount of magical power, as I had strength and size... surely that meant amazing things.

I pulled on my cotton pajamas, my skin still hot from my shower, and sat on the couch in my small living room. My hands were warm and buzzing with an energy I'd never felt before. I had to know; I simply had to.

While my magic wasn't terrible, I'd never been good at anything. I'd barely gotten through high school, thanks to almost failing the classes in spells and potions. But what was I truly dreadful at?

The answer came to me easily. Magical jewelry-making.

To be fair, that wasn't just me, it was pretty much everyone at my school. Anyone who wasn't meant to be a craftsman, or metal-smith, couldn't make jewelry the magical way. It just wasn't done.

Only three people had passed metal-smithing class, and they all went on to become jewelers.

"What do I need in the way of jewelry?" I asked aloud, rubbing my hands together. I rarely wore jewelry of any sort. No rings or necklaces, and I only kept a pair of gold studs in my ears so the holes wouldn't close up.

My mother had pierced them when I was three years old because she loved sparkles. I'd never had the heart to let them go completely, even though I still never changed out the gold for the sparkles Mom had always wanted for me.

"Something for Mom, then." I smiled at the thought. My mother deserved the best of everything.

I closed my eyes and put my hands out, stretching and wiggling my fingers to let the magic flow. In my mind I could see a gorgeous gold necklace. Mom's favorite color was green, so I imagined a large emerald centerpiece, hanging off a sturdy gold chain.

Yes, that looks pretty.

My hands warmed and magic flowed through me. I smiled

wider, enjoying the exercise even though I fully expected to open my eyes and see nothing there. Or at most, a mangled piece of metal that resembled nothing like what I envisaged.

When the warmth of my magic flow slowed and then stopped, I opened my eyes to see what my ridiculous imagination had pretended I could create.

I stared down at the coffee table in shock. "It can't be." I was hallucinating now, surely?

I reached out and picked up the gorgeous necklace lying in front of me on the table. The metal was slightly warm to the touch, and heavy. And the piece was utterly beautiful. "Oh, my... God."

It was real. The links were gold and the emerald was huge and sparkling, even in the dim light of my apartment. I turned the piece this way and that, inspecting it like I expected it to disappear any minute.

But the necklace didn't disappear. Instead, it got colder and more settled in my hands.

Carefully, I put it down on the table, got up and walked away.

This wasn't possible. No... way.

I put myself to bed, but after an hour of not being able to fall asleep, I went and got the necklace, put it on the pillow next to me, and stared at it.

Was this real? Was it possible that my magic had improved? Gotten stronger and more powerful?

Was it truly possible that Harry's dying wish had actually come true?

I forced myself to close my eyes but it was hours before I actually fell asleep. Only time would tell if this was just some sort of weird trick. Or my new reality.

THE NEXT DAY I fronted up for the afternoon shift, grief still present but my heart was lighter than it had been in a while.

"Tania! You're back!" Jaydy hurried up to the reception desk, a big smile on her face. "You'll never guess what!"

"What?" I asked, grinning at the big, strong woman I'd known for so long. She was a lovely person, and her beautiful nature shone through in her eyes. "You here to set another personal best?" I asked her, when she didn't respond straight away.

Jaydy held lots of records in her weight division and was a fantastic example of a strong, fit, healthy power lifter.

She laughed. "Yeah, I'm competing next month, but that's not what's awesome. I just got the Potions Master job at our old high school."

My jaw dropped. "But you... they..."

She grinned at me, totally understanding where my thoughts had gone. "I know, right? They only ever pick the very best, and I've never been known for my magic. Especially potions. But I just had this strong feeling that I wanted to give it a go, and somehow I blitzed at the interview. I couldn't believe it."

I stared at her, shocked. Was it possible that Harry's wish had spread wider than simply me? Had the genie wish filtered down to affect all supernatural women like me? Big. Strong. Voluptuous and chubby.

Was our magic now equal to our size? Wonder filled my chest. Then I realized I hadn't said anything about her announcement.

"Congratulations Jaydy," I managed, still feeling shocked. "It's great news. You work so hard at everything, and you really deserve it."

She headed off into the gym, speaking over her shoulder as she went. "Not really, but I'm still rapt! Thanks Tania!"

I watched her disappear into the gym, my heart filled with joy. If this was possible. if this was really happening...

Oh... this is awesome!

Ever the realist, I still wanted an independent person to give me an opinion. I could just be fooling myself here.

When George arrived for his nightly training session, as he always did at six p.m., I walked over to greet him.

"Hey George."

"Hey Tania. Heard your parents bought a place in town."

I laughed, because if I ever thought I was going to surprise George, I was wrong. "Is there anything you don't know?"

He shrugged. "I don't know what's going on with you right now. Something's up. What is it?"

I swallowed hard. "I was hoping you wouldn't mind hanging round for an hour to spot me?"

His eyebrows climbed his forehead. "Pushing some upper limits?"

I nodded. "Yeah. That okay with you?" I usually trained alone. I was smart about my weights and had good technique, and I never worried about the fact I didn't have a partner.

George grinned broadly. "Of course. I'll get something to eat now, and push back my work-out an hour. Then I can be done in time with your shift ending." He winked, turned tail and headed out the door again.

I waved, nervous excitement filling my belly. It couldn't be true. Surely. But everything inside of me was excited, and I couldn't shake the feeling that something fundamental had changed inside of me.

I finished my shift and closed the computer down. George had eaten and was now in the back, training hard. I changed the music to something more my style, a little lighter and more dance-oriented. I could practically hear his groan even before he released it.

"Oh. Shut up," I called out. "Just gonna change. Will be back in five."

I rushed upstairs to my apartment, threw on some workout clothes and came down to train with George, not sure what we were might both be about to discover.

FOUR

My heart was pumping a little harder, excitement warring with apprehension in my head. What if I was wrong about the genie power? Hopefully I wasn't about to tear a muscle or hurt my back.

"So, what are we starting with?" George called, grabbing his dark towel and wiping his sweat-covered face.

"Maximum dead lifts."

George frowned. "You haven't warmed up yet."

I walked over to the bar, setting the weight to forty pounds heavier than I'd ever lifted before. Suicide for any normal person.

"Please, George. Just trust me on this. Spot me. Okay?"

He groaned and moved into place to catch the bar if I needed him. "Fine. But when you do your back, just know, my healing fees are not cheap!"

I bent my knees and reached for the bar. My fingers wrapped around the metal pole and I grabbed on tight, centering myself and getting ready to lift.

My magic surged inside me, powerful and far stronger than it had ever been in the past.

I pushed my weight into my heels, brought the bar up my body, took a breath, then exhaled as I pushed it above my head.

There was no strain. No pain. No tension, even.

It was as easy as lifting my washing basket above my head. I laughed. Then dropped it like it was nothing.

The thump of the heavy weights against the mat made a loud noise, and I twisted around to grin up at George. "That was awesome."

George was gaping at me. He didn't speak, simply walked up to the weights, and slid on forty more pounds.

I frowned. Wasn't that a step too far? "Seriously? I just did a personal best, George. I was happy to leave it there."

He chuckled. "You did that easily. Stop fooling around and lift something."

I couldn't believe he was pushing me to lift something so heavy. I added up the weight and shook my head. Half the power-lifting men I knew wouldn't lift this weight at all.

"Fine." I huffed, as I got into position once more, bending my knees and tucking my ass super low to the ground.

I rallied my strength, but my muscles wouldn't budge. They strained against the heaviness of the weight. That was, they strained until I reached for my magic When the surge went through me, bolstering my body, I was suddenly able to lift the bar above my head.

Not so easy that time. But I'd done it, and I hadn't pulled or torn a single muscle.

Sweat dripped down my face, and when I dropped the bar, it was to the sound of George clapping.

I was panting as I turned to him.

"How the hell did you do that?" he asked, his eyes wide. "Even with your magic, I didn't think you could do something like that."

I laughed and panted, and laughed some more, and finally, I shook my head. "It's the wish. It has to be." Part of me couldn't believe it, but I'd also long ago realized that magic and love could do truly amazing things.

Thank you, Harry, I silently whispered. *I wish you were here to enjoy this with me.*

George crossed his big meaty arms over his chest, suspicion etched on his face. "The wish? What do you mean?"

I needed to tell someone I trusted as the secret was beginning to weigh heavily on me. So, I explained to George about what had happened with Harry, and what I'd wished as a teen. Then about the necklace I'd made, and the magic currently simmering in my veins. Power I'd never experienced before.

When I was done, George's eyes were comically wide, and his arms had dropped to his sides. "You mean... the more you train, the stronger you'll be, and the more magic you'll have?"

I shrugged. "I have no idea how it works. All I know is that I already train hard. I'm pretty strong, not to toot my own horn. But for a woman..."

"You're top level. We know that, Tania. Magic wishes aside, that's why we all want to see you compete."

I waved my hand in a dismissive gesture. "That's not what I meant. It's more that I finally feel like my magic is as strong as my body. I've never thought that before. In fact, it's never been the case."

George frowned. "I don't understand."

"I... I think my magic is far stronger than it ever was. I feel more powerful, in every way."

"Well, do something." George said, inviting me with a gesture at the room. "Go for it."

I grinned at him. "You mean, other than lifting what I just did? Okay." I turned to face the small shop at the side of the gym, the one where we sold protein shakes, powders, and gym equipment like hand weights and yoga mats. I extended my hands out, then flicked my arms down.

All of the shop blinds rolled down at speed, unfurling at a rate of knots.

"Oh, come on." George scoffed. "Put some effort into it."

I huffed. Didn't he realize that a week ago I wouldn't have been able to do even that? My magic really had been very minimal. But I'd never been one to back down from a challenge, so I threw my practical magic at the area next to me, conjuring up a large table, and a full banquet-style dinner. Meats. Bread. Fruits and bottles of wine. Sparkling glasses and shiny silver cutlery. With a fancy pattern I conjured out of my imagination.

George grunted. He was still pretending not to be impressed, but I could tell he was shaken. "Make some more equipment," he said, gesturing to the benches and weights around us.

I inhaled sharply. That was a lot of mass. A lot of magic required.

I didn't stop. I twisted my fingers and spoke an incantation for creating objects inside my mind, putting effort and force into conjuring up dumb-bells the size of my head.

"Wow," George whispered, reaching down to touch one of the dumb-bells and pick it up.

His biceps bulged as he flexed his arm. "Nice and solid. Wow. Seriously, Tania. I didn't know you had this sort of magic."

I conjured up a chair next to the dining table and sat down, panting with exertion. "I didn't before. I practically failed most of my magical exams at school, George. I'm not powerful at all. I run a gym for a reason." I gestured to the shop and warehouse space around us.

George magicked up his own chair, larger and stronger than mine for his huge bulk, then collapsed onto it. "Well, you are now."

I swiveled around so my legs were under the table and I could look straight at my friend and fellow warlock. "I am. And it's not just me. My wish was to help all witches like me. All the bigger girls."

"Power lifters?" he clarified.

I shook my head. "Not really. I was thinking more about size, not strength. I wasn't this strong in high school, but I was big. Tall. Overweight. And I wanted to be powerful to match my size, in magic and physically."

George reached for a chicken leg, looking pleased when it proved to be real. "Well, it looks like you got your wish," he said, before taking a huge bite of the chicken meat.

His words filtered over me and I heaved a massive sigh to let out some of the emotion that swirled deep inside me. It was a big thing to process. "Yeah, I suppose I did." I reached for a bread roll and picked up the knife stuck in golden butter.

We ate for a short while, sitting in companionable silence while we devoured half the food. Power lifters consumed food like no other person. I'd always loved to eat, and watching my dad put away a whole cooked chicken and most of a roast lamb leg was a regular Sunday afternoon occurrence.

Eating with George was the same, and I found myself relaxing at the familiarity of it all.

"Hey, I've asked my dad to help train some of the more elite lifters. Would you be up for a few sessions with an old footballer?"

George's jaw dropped. "Are you serious? Of course, I bloody would."

I smiled, "I'm glad. Dad would like that."

There was another short silence, then George said, "Hey... I've got some friends looking for a witch. Do you want some more work?"

I cocked my head at him. "Work? What sort of work?"

And what sort of 'friends' needed a witch?

George looked down at his plate. "They need a powerful witch to alter a curse, I think. I told them I'd ask around, but I didn't have anyone in mind to ask... until now."

"And you think I can help them?" I was shocked George was even mentioning it.

I didn't sell my magic. I'd always thought of myself first and foremost as a business owner. A single, independent woman, but not particularly magical. I was not hired out for magical skills, abilities, or spells. The concept was new to me.

"Who are these friends?" I asked.

George still wasn't looking at me, which meant he was uncomfortable about answering the question.

"Well... they're other supernaturals." He coughed and cleared his throat, and I immediately went on guard.

There was only one type of supernatural that warlocks and witches didn't mess with. "They're wolf shifters, aren't they?"

George lifted his head and met my gaze. "Yeah. They are. So I would understand if you don't want to consider the job."

I sat back in my chair, my belly full. I was physically replete, but feeling a little confused. "Since when do you associate with shifters, George?"

He shrugged. "They're good guys, mostly. I had a run in with some bear shifters a few years ago, and these wolves saved my ass. Been friends with them ever since."

It was my turn to be surprised. The shifters and the magicals had a natural enemy status that I'd never thought much about. Shifters lived on the other side of town, in the south, and I'd rarely seen one in real life.

The once or twice I'd bumped into one, they'd met my gaze, realized I was a low-grade witch, and kept on walking.

But in this case, there was only one answer, "Of course I'll help your friends, George. If they helped you, I'd be happy to assist them."

I had questions about how they'd saved his ass. George wasn't a man to lose a fight, so those bear shifters must have been mean bastards.

George's smile was brilliant as he dragged himself up to his feet. "Okay. I'll get in contact with them, and let you know."

He thanked me for the food, and headed off.

I pulled my magic to the forefront of my mind, then cleaned up all the food and the table and chairs, with a single swipe of my arm. That was pretty cool, I had to admit.

I went upstairs to have a shower and went to bed with a smile on my face. My life had just taken a massive turn for the better.

But as I let myself relax into my pillow on the verge of sleep, the hairs on my arms prickled with premonition.

Something strange, this way blows.

FIVE

I glanced at the huge sign stretching above my head, then slid my gaze to my brother, Leo. "Are you sure this is the place?"

We were standing in front of a gym that reeked of testosterone and human stench.

"That's what George said." Leo nodded his head at the door, then pushed on the glass panel. "So, let's do this."

He charged through the door and disappeared inside, and I stared after him. "Shit."

This wasn't where I wanted to be. Asking a witch for help was the last thing I wanted.

"Come on, dickhead," Leo called through the rapidly closing door.

I rolled my eyes heavenward, and pushed inside after him. The stench hit me like a fucking wall. Piss and sweat, with a strong wave of ammonia cleaning products beneath it all.

Sometimes being a wolf shifter and having enhanced senses had a down side.

"Hey, how you doin'?" Leo asked the pretty girl behind the counter.

She smiled back, but seemed unmoved by my brother's charm, which was impressive. Most of the women we met practically fell at his feet.

"I'm good, sir. Can I help you?"

"We're looking for Tania," Leo said.

Her features immediately shuttered. "Tania isn't here at the moment. Can I give her a message?"

Leo went to speak, but I pressed forward, taking over the conversation. "If she's around, could you tell her that we're here? George sent us. We're old friends of his."

Something must have connected, because she nodded and said, "Let me go and speak to someone. Will you wait here?"

Leo said, "Thanks."

I turned away and wandered around the foyer. There were rows and rows of supplements, and racks of clothes.

So human.

I shuddered. What was this super-powerful witch doing owning a mostly human gym? Made no sense at all.

"Are you sure this is where George told us to find her?" I whispered when Leo joined me at one of the clothing racks.

George had been a friend for a long time, ever since Leo and I had found the huge warlock receiving a hiding from a pack of four bear shifters. He'd been holding his own against them, an impressive feat considering their strength and numbers, but he wouldn't have lasted much longer without taking some major damage.

We'd stepped in and turned the tide for him. Something I would have done for anyone in the same circumstances.

But George hadn't simply walked away. He'd made us friends and drinking buddies. He was a decent man and we liked and respected him.

Leo nodded. "Yep. I'm sure. Oh, my... fucking... *hell*..." Leo began shaking like a leaf.

I grabbed his arm. "What's happened? What's wrong with you?"

Leo's eyes were wide, his pupils dilated and had turned silver with his wolf shifter.

I shook him hard. "Stop it." There were rules about exposing ourselves to humans. And there were way too many of them around here to risk shifting.

Leo pointed behind me, without speaking. I turned around, a growl in my throat. Who was this enemy that had turned my brother into a shivering zombie version of himself?

The moment I fixed my gaze on the other side of the room, I saw her.

She was the most beautiful woman I'd ever encountered. Her curves were sumptuous. Her long dark hair gleamed with good health and her face... An angel had fallen.

"I..." I couldn't get any words out. My heart was too heavy in my chest. My mouth was dry and I had to force myself to swallow.

The heavenly woman walked toward us, her lips curved up in a welcoming smile.

As she got closer, I realized she was still looking me in the eyes, a very rare moment for me. I was over six foot four, and this woman had to be six foot herself. And at least two hundred pounds.

I couldn't wait to throw her down onto my bed... any bed, and ravage her. Where were these thoughts coming from? But I couldn't help myself.

"Hi. I'm Tania. Are you the guys George said were looking for some help?"

She didn't seem at all affected by our presence. Whereas my

heart was pounding like I'd shifted under a full moon and was running full pelt through the woods.

Leo seemed similarly affected. Even worse than me, he didn't seem to be able to speak at all.

I nodded, because it seemed a safe response.

She took a step back and gestured for us to follow. "Why don't we chat in my office. It's pretty loud out here."

We followed her like lost little puppies through the huge gym, with men and women alike lifting huge weights and grunting out their frustrations and triumphs.

From the smell, most of them were human. I noticed another witch, and two warlocks. No other shifters though.

Tania led us to a small room at the back of the gym. As soon as we walked inside, the smell of the human men lifted, and her scent became more distinct. More potent.

I gasped at the effect her scent had on my body. My cock hardened and I couldn't stop the flush of arousal sweeping through my body.

Tania walked over to sit behind a desk, and I rushed forward to sit on the chair opposite her.

Leo was right behind me.

"So," Tania said, all business as she slid forward in her chair behind the desk. "George told me you're looking for someone to break a curse. I have no idea if I can help, but I'm certainly willing to try."

"Thank you," I managed to spit out, then coughed to clear my throat.

Tania's dark eyebrows drew together in concern. "Are you guys okay?"

Leo cleared his throat and finally managed to get his voice working. "Yes, we just... aren't used to so many humans. The smell..."

Tania's eyes widened, then she chuckled softly, the sound as musical as harp strings. *So beautiful.*

"Oh yes, I see. I'd forgotten that shifters had heightened senses, I apologize. Would you like to move our meeting somewhere else?"

The fact she'd offered, and seemed like she actually cared about our comfort, said a lot about her naturally caring nature.

"No," I managed to grunt out, knowing it was her and not all the humans out in the gym who had caused this reaction in Leo and me. No matter where we held our meeting, we'd likely be the same. "In here is fine."

Tania leaned back in her chair, arms crossed over her plain t-shirt and ample breasts. I tried not to be creepy and let my gaze dwell on her curves, but my fingers itched to reach out and gently caress her. *All of her. Every sexy inch.*

"Tell me how I can help you."

I glanced over at Leo, who nodded at me to explain. I sucked in a deep breath and took my time explaining our predicament. "When we were kids, our parents were cursed by a witch."

Tania's gaze slid from me to Leo, then back again. "You're brothers?"

"Yes."

She smiled softly. "I can kind of see a resemblance. Not much though."

Leo shrugged. "We don't look alike. I took after Mom."

"And I look like our father," I explained, though it hardly seemed necessary to the story. "Anyway. Our parents are trapped in their wolf forms, and have been for almost twenty years."

Tania's eyes shimmered with sudden, unexpected tears. "Oh my... how did that happen?"

I shrugged. "We don't know. I was about fifteen and Leo was only thirteen when it happened. They just disappeared overnight.

When we found them in their shifter forms, and they didn't change back over the weeks that followed, we put the story together, piece by piece."

Leo slid forward on his seat and said, "From what we've put together, our parents must have done something to piss off a powerful witch. What, we don't know, because they weren't the sort of people to look for trouble."

"Quite the opposite," I said. "Mom was a schoolteacher and Dad a mechanic."

Tania nodded, then stood up and walked over to a book shelf in the corner. "So, you need help reversing the spell and making them human again?"

"Yes. If it's possible?"

She ran her finger along the bookshelf and frowned. "Why did you guys wait so long, if you don't mind me asking?"

I glanced at Leo. We had an answer to that question, but I wasn't sure if she was going to like it.

Leo's lips twisted as he said. "We didn't realize it was a witch's doing for a long time, then when we spoke to people, like George, they said that such a curse couldn't be reversed."

Tania twisted to look at us, one hand on her hip. "But George sent you to me anyway."

"Yes. He said you're more powerful than him, and since my parents have returned to the city for a short time, he thought maybe you could help."

She bit her lip and chewed on the luscious body part.

Damn, I wish I could sink my teeth into her as well...

"They go away for long periods of time?" she asked.

Leo answered, because I was too busy trying to get my cock to settle down.

"Yeah, sometimes for months. Longer."

She sighed, and the heaviness of her sadness filtered over and touched me. "I'm so sorry. I couldn't imagine being without my parents."

Leo shrugged. "We had our pack, and each other."

Tania walked toward the spiral staircase and took a step up. "I have to find a specific book, and it's upstairs. Can you guys wait here a minute?"

I nodded and gulped at the way her ass curved and how sexy her legs looked in that position.

They will feel so good wrapped around my waist while I'm driving into her...

"Yes! Of course!" I managed, then she turned tail and ran up the stairs and disappeared.

Leo shot to his feet and gasped out at me. "Oh my fucking God, I think she's my mate! But how is that possible? I thought all our mates were meant to be fated? Wolves. Oh... *shit.*"

Leo was running his hands through his hair, looking frazzled and truly shaken.

I got to my feet as well, and turned to face him, a preternatural stillness falling over me. I had to force myself to swallow the inhuman growl that rose from my chest and focus on not ripping my brother's throat out.

I tried once, but the words failed to come. I tried again, taking a deep breath first, then finally saying the one thing I never expected to utter. "That's impossible, Leo. She can't be *your* fated mate. Because she's mine."

I glared at my brother, the anger rising in my gut so fast my wolf struggled to process all the emotions. My chest was heavy with tension and my fingers tightened into fists.

"That's... no. She can't be." It didn't make sense. "We can't have the same fated mate."

Mason began to pace up and down the small office, growling like a caged animal. "Well obviously we can. Because whatever you're feeling, I've got it just as bad. I can barely breathe." He dropped his voice to a whisper. "And my cock has a mind of its own. It wants me to throw her down on the desk and claim her the second she gets her luscious ass back here."

I growled softly at my brother to tell him exactly what I thought of that idea, but since I knew she'd be back any minute, I tried to lighten the mood a little by grasping onto humor.

"Hey, speaking of her ass." I waggled my eyebrows. "Isn't she enough woman for the both of us?"

Mason stared at me, then cracked a reluctant smile. "You think that's why she's so big?"

"Why who is so big?" Tania asked, jogging down the stairs with a huge book in her arms.

"Nothing," I mumbled. "What did you find?"

Tania reached the bottom of the stairs and tugged on her t-shirt as though she was trying to cover her ass. "My dad's an NFL player. I got his physique. It's not my fault I'm bigger and stronger than most men."

I gaped at her. Despite the surface calm of her voice, I could hear the pain behind the words. To my ears, she sounded hurt and defensive.

She placed the magic book on the desk and stared at the front cover as though she'd see the answer to all of life's questions within the folds of the leather. But it was obvious that she didn't want to look at me. And I couldn't have that.

"What are you talking about?" I managed. "You're fucking beautiful."

Her head came up so fast, her gaze pinned me in place. She seemed to search my eyes for the truth, with a silent question about why I lied.

I stared back, trying to tell her with my gaze that I wasn't lying. That I wanted her. And that she was gorgeous. Just as she was.

Big. And strong. And fucking to-die-for beautiful.

She dropped her gaze away first and sat in the chair again, opening her magic book as though I hadn't spoken.

I glanced over at my brother. Had she just ignored my words? Didn't she understand what I was saying?

"Tania..."

"Leo. Sit," she barked, her tone sharp. "Let's see if I can help you with your parents and the spell."

Mason and I sat down again, but I couldn't believe she was ignoring what I'd said. Worst of all, she seemed immune to the feelings of the fated mate bond that had overpowered Mason and me.

I wanted her, so badly. I had since the first moment I'd laid eyes on her. It sounded so contrite and bullshit, but the stories about fated mates were so right.

My friends, my family, my pack... they'd told me since I was young that the moment I saw my mate, I'd know. That the whole world would shift around me, centering my entire focus on the woman made for me.

To have her be a witch was one thing. But to share her with my brother? I wasn't sure I could do that.

"Okay, so..." Her finger traced over the pages of an ancient book. "It's quite hard to undo a spell done by another witch or warlock. It's much better if that magical being lifts the curse themselves. But you two don't know who cursed your parents, do you?"

She lifted her head and none of the heat I felt, or acknowledgment of us, was there in her dark eyes.

I shook my head. "No. We don't."

"Hmmm...." Tania went back to reading and I sat and waited.

Mason's knee bounced up and down, a sign of his impatience. Tania didn't seem to notice. She just skimmed over page after page until finally she stopped. "Ah-ha! I think I've found something."

I slid forward and reached for the edge of the desk that felt like a deliberate buffer she'd placed between us. "What is it?"

"There is a spell to lift a curse like you're talking about. It's complicated and pretty full on. But I'd be willing to try it." She looked up, with a satisfied smile on her face.

I steeled myself for the next words about payment, but they didn't come.

I glanced at Mason, who in turn looked at Tania and said,

"That's the other reason we've put this off finding a witch for so long. We've been told the payment for such a spell would be more than we could afford. But we've both been saving money, we have property…"

Hell, we had two livers, four kidneys… whatever she needed. We'd hand them all over if it meant getting our parents back.

Her eyes widened, then she cracked another huge grin. "I don't charge for my magic."

It was our turn to be shocked. "You don't? No. That's impossible."

She laughed, and once again, the sound was music to my ears. "I've never had anyone hire me to do a spell for them. I wouldn't even know what to charge."

I looked around the room. She owned this business, so she probably owned the building too. She didn't need money. Or did she?

I sat up straight, willing to put an offer on the table even though Mason and I had agreed we would be careful what we said in this regard. "Whatever you think is fair, Tania. We'll pay it. Anything."

"Anything?" She sounded interested.

I nodded. "Yes. Anything." I wasn't scared of what she would ask for. She didn't seem like the type of woman who would take for the sake of taking.

She tilted her head as though considering something strange, then shook herself. "No. I don't want anything."

"Do you need more people in the gym?" Mason offered. "We can promote you to all the shifter groups. Or if you want cash, we have cash."

He pulled out his wallet and lay it on the table, something else we'd promised not to do.

The wallet was bulging with cash, and although Tania probably didn't realize that all of the notes were one-hundred-dollar bills, the thickness of the wallet was still impressive.

Tania sighed. "You both need to know that I might not succeed with this spell. If I'm not strong enough... or if something goes wrong..."

Mason hastened to say, "The fact you're willing to try, is more than enough for us."

"I'll tell you what." Her smile softened. "If my dad likes you, the spell's free."

I blinked at her. That was the weirdest request ever.

"And if he doesn't?" I asked.

She shrugged. "If I succeed in getting your parents back... you can join the gym, both of you, and pay your fees, just like everyone else."

Her generosity made my heart ache.

I opened my mouth to thank her, and she put her hand up, effectively silencing me. "Don't thank me yet, I haven't done anything except agree to try."

I nodded and stood up, extending my hand out to her. "And I thank you for being willing to try, for meeting with us."

She eyed my hand like I might be holding a buzzer or something equally juvenile, then stood up and shook it.

Tingles of awareness shot up my arm and I had to lock my knees so I didn't stumble.

Stop being a pussy. Harden up.

She turned to shake Mason's hand, then we thanked her again, and left. She didn't follow us. In fact, she closed the office door behind us.

I managed to get out of the gym, and onto the footpath before my wolf shifter howled to the sky. "I need to run."

Mason nodded. "Me too. Let's go."

We jumped into our truck and sped off home. We'd shift and

run through the forest, and tonight we'd explain to our parents what we'd done.

Not only had we found a witch powerful enough to at least try and help them, but my brother and I had found our mate.

It was just a pity she didn't seem to know it yet.

I pressed my back against the office door and slid to the floor in a pile of female weakness. Thank God I'd managed to hold it together until the wolf shifters left.

I wanted them. Both of them. My belly was tight, my pussy throbbing with need.

Seriously. What the hell was wrong with me? I'd never desired men on sight before, and certainly not two gorgeous brothers who wouldn't want anything to do with a woman like me.

They'd want what every man wanted. Someone like my mother. Petite. Blonde. Dainty. Beautiful.

The fact that they'd even remotely tried to defend themselves when I heard them laughing about how big my ass was, lessened the insult a little. And even though Leo didn't *seem* to be lying when he said I was beautiful, I didn't believe him.

They needed something from me, and they were the type of guys who would do anything to get it.

Like they'd said. Literally anything was on the table. Money. Property. Probably even a night or two in their bed.

I shivered at the very idea of what those men would be able to do between the sheets. I'd never had a good lover before. Sure, I'd dated and had a boyfriend or two, but the fireworks people spoke about? I'd never experienced them.

BOB was the only thing that had ever induced an orgasm in me. My battery-operated boyfriend. He was the best. He never failed me.

But I was pretty sure those wolf shifters could easily change my mind about what constituted a good lover.

I hauled myself up from the floor and forced myself to pick up the spell book and climb the stairs once more to my apartment. Once I got there, I sat on my couch and went through the incantation once more.

It was a difficult spell. There was no getting around that fact. And I honestly wouldn't have even attempted it a few weeks ago. But if I trained hard for a few weeks, and boosted my magic, there was a possibility I could do it.

When they'd asked me to help them, I'd been so flattered, I could barely talk right. Or maybe that had been the animal magnetism I'd suffered under.

I'd never spent any time with wolf shifters, and only dated humans or warlocks. It had never even crossed my mind to try to meet other types of supernaturals.

I sighed as I placed the book down, and lay down on the couch.

Damn, those men were beautiful.

There was no way they'd ever go for a woman like me, so I needed to stay strong, and make sure they didn't see how I felt. I was actually proud of the way I'd dealt with them. Coolly. Professionally.

I'd had to deal with a lot of good-looking men before, of course. I owned a gym after all. But I'd never been so attracted to any man before, let alone two at once. And brothers!

"Oh, my mother would die if she knew."

And almost as if I'd conjured her, I heard my mother's voice call out. "Darling? Are you up there?"

I sighed and pushed up from the couch. My parents were in my office, directly below me. "Yeah, I'm upstairs. Come on up."

Heavy footsteps sounded on the spiral staircase as Dad stomped up and Mom flew. "Tania!" Mom cried, launching herself at me.

I caught her and laughed, hugging her tight. "Did you guys pick up the keys to the new place?"

Dad held them up, the old-fashioned silver keys dangling from his big fingers. "Yep. Picked them up today."

"We stopped by here on our way. We thought you might wanna come with us."

They were looking at me so expectantly, I couldn't refuse. "Sure. I'd love to."

"You don't have to work?" Dad asked, ever the responsible one.

I shook my head. "They'll be fine without me for a few hours." I grabbed my keys and my cell, then followed my parents back down the staircase and into the gym.

Dad stood in the middle of the room, slowly turning around, surveying his handiwork. "Could use a new coat of paint."

I glanced up at the ceiling, where his focus was. "It looks great still, Dad."

He shook his head. "The flow isn't quite right, either. I think I can optimize the work out space better if I move some things around for you."

I laughed, happy for him to help. I would never have gotten this place without my parents' support. They'd helped me every step of the way. "You can change anything you want, Dad. You know I trust you."

And I did. Something I loved about my life was that I could trust my parents to do the right thing by me. A lot of my friends didn't have that luxury. And then there were those like the wolf shifters who'd had their parents stolen from them.

I let Sherrie at the front desk know that I'd be out for a while, and we headed outside to my parents' massive truck. With my father's height and weight, he didn't fit into normal vehicles.

Once we were in, and driving to the new place, I decided to ask Mom about the spell. "Hey, Mom. Can I get your opinion on something?"

"Of course."

"A friend of mine, George—you'll be meeting him, Dad. He's a warlock, and one of the best power lifters at the gym."

Dad nodded, and I continued. "Well, he has some friends, some wolfs shifters, who came to me for help with a spell."

Mom's intake of breath told me everything I needed to know about her feelings toward wolf shifters.

"You can't help them," Dad ground out.

I sighed. "I've already said I would. They saved George's life a few years ago, and he owes them."

"But *you* don't," Mom reminded me.

At that point we arrived at the house. I glanced out the window to see an historic home that was falling into disrepair. But it had lovely lines, and a nice energy to it. "It's really beautiful."

Dad laughed. "Hardly. But it will be once I'm done with it."

We got out of the car and Mom slid her hand around my arm. "We don't help shifters, Tania."

I wanted to roll my eyes, but managed to stop myself in time. "Mom. Their parents were cursed to be wolves, forever. By a witch. They can't shift back. These two guys, brothers, have practically raised themselves. They just want their parents back. How can I not help them with something as fundamental as that?"

Mom's eyebrows drew together, but she didn't say anything.

Dad stomped off to the front door, out of ear shot.

Mom turned to me. "What's your question?"

"I found a spell I think might help, but I know the best way of lifting the curse would be to find the witch who put it there in the first place."

Mom nodded. "Yes, it would be."

"So, do I do a location spell first? What do you suggest?"

Mom tilted her head to the side, thinking. "How long's this curse been on the parents?"

I shrugged. Leo and Mason looked to be in their early to mid-thirties, and they said they'd been alone since they were teens. "Fifteen to twenty years, at a guess."

Mom grimaced. "Then it's doubtful the witch would be willing to lift it even if you could find her, or him. That's a long time not to see your children."

Mom was beginning to empathize with their situation now, which was a good sign. I wasn't changing my mind about helping them, so it would be good to have Mom on side, too.

"So, what do I do?"

Dad called out to us. "Come on you two."

Mom tugged me toward the house. 'I'll help you, if you want. When you meet up with the wolf parents, I'll do a location spell and see if the witch is still alive. If she isn't, the spell will be a lot easier to break."

I grinned at her as we walked up to their new house. "Thanks Mom." She was willing to lend her magic to my cause, which was lovely of her.

Should I tell her that I didn't need the help, that I could likely now do such a spell on my own?

My mother was a thin, beautiful, classical witch with lots of power. I'd never surpassed her in levels, or magical ability, before. Was it now possible that I could I top her?

We entered the house and the smell was the first thing that hit me. The dust was so thick the air was clogged with it. White sheets covered old furniture and the stained flowery carpet was thick with grime.

Beneath it all though, I could see the potential. The stained-glass windows, the marble fireplace. If anyone could bring an old mansion like this back from the brink, it was my parents with a combination of magic and sheer hard work.

I coughed and sneezed, laughing as I said, "No-one's lived here for a while, I see."

Mom clapped her hands and whispered a cleaning spell. The white sheets lifted off the furniture, then disappeared from sight. Next came an army of brooms, dustpans, feather dusters and vacuums. One of each appeared in each room that I could see, moving of their own volition.

I grinned at Mom, who shrugged in an unapologetic fashion. She didn't lift a finger for cleaning. Deemed it a waste of her time.

"Come see the upstairs," Dad said, carefully taking one step at a time up the gorgeous wooden staircase.

Mom chuckled. "Be careful. I'm not sure about the stability of these floors."

We walked up the stairs, slowly. At the top was a long hallway with many bedrooms and two large, ancient bathrooms branching off the hall.

"You're gonna need more than a cleaning spell for this bath-room," I called out to Mom as I stuck my head in to the room and took in the black and white seventies remodel. It was a nice space but definitely in need of a knockdown.

Mom shrugged. "So your father gets to take a sledge hammer to some walls. He'll just call it a work out."

"Sure will be," Dad called out from the other end of the house.

I spent a little more time with my parents at their new house, *oohing* and *aahing* over the potential while my mother used her magic to at least make it clean enough to live in while they began their renovations of the mansion.

"I hope you'll choose some of the décor," Mom said as she was kissing me goodbye. "I want you to have a bedroom here too, if you ever want to stay here."

I laughed. "You're within walking distance of my place, Mom."

Dad slung a huge arm over my mom's petite shoulders. "Yeah, but if we decide to head back to the country for a while, you could always stay here. Have some more space. That apartment of yours is bloody small for someone with our genetics."

Then it hit me. My parents were trying to give me a house that I couldn't afford.

"You guys aren't doing this for me... are you?"

Their faces showed twin looks of shock, then denial. "Oh well, we just wanted to be closer to you," Mom said.

I gave them a side eye, then just laughed. As their only child I'd always been spoiled, but within the realms of reasonable. Renovating a massive house for me, was going a step too far. I would never accept it.

But telling them that was crazy too. My dad's stubborn streak was as wide as his arm span. "I love you guys. I'm so glad you've moved to town."

We said goodbye and despite my dad's offer to drive me back, I decided to walk. My legs ached from training hard last night and I wanted to stretch them out a little. As I navigated through the streets and headed back to my gym, I couldn't help but think about the fact that my life had changed so dramatically in the past few days.

Time would tell if I was right about my suspicions in relation to Harry's final words, and if the extra power really was the gift it seemed, or a curse.

EIGHT

MASON

My jaw remained clenched so tight, my teeth ached. And my wolf vibrated within my chest, anxious and desperate to jump free. "I am so fucking sick of waiting."

I'd found my mate and I couldn't even go and see her or talk to her. And God, did I want to do more than just talk to her. I wanted to ravish her. Strip her down and devour her.

Leo, the bloody sloth, laughed at me from his place on the couch. "We've found the witch to save Mom and Dad, and she wants no money? It's a bloody miracle. After years of saving every cent and waiting for the day someone would want to help us, we should be celebrating, Mason. Not fucking bitching."

I growled at my brother and hauled myself out of the old recliner I sat in. We'd done everything we could over the last ten years, to make money to help our parents. We bought old houses and did them up, sold them for a profit.

We saved money like our lives depended on it, because our parents' lives actually did.

We both had old cars and ancient furniture—and not the expensive kind. We crammed ourselves into a tiny townhouse and didn't bother renovating it because we were too busy working to pay off the mortgage.

"I can't believe we don't need the money we got told we did!" I paced the tiny room, feeling claustrophobic.

We had a fucking fortune in the bank, ready to buy our parents their freedom. And the only witch who would agree to help us wanted us to join her gym for a couple hundred bucks a year?

It was elating. But I couldn't fully enjoy that development, because my wolf was howling to go fetch my mate. His mate. *Our* mate.

That was the most frustrating thing of all. I did not want to share my mate with my brother. But it looked as if fate had a different take on my future than I'd had.

Leo picked up his phone and started scrolling, obviously needing a brainless activity to occupy him. "So, we have money. We can send Mom and Dad on a world trip now, or buy them a nice house to retire in. When they're human again. We can help them properly."

I flopped down into the old recliner again, the springs creaking in protest. "Yeah. I suppose." Leo was right. I should be jumping for joy, but instead, my skin itched to be scratched right off.

I jumped out of the chair again, unable to sit still. "I've gotta go and see her."

Leo was on his feet faster than a whip. "I'm coming with you."

"Oh, so you're not as relaxed as you're pretending to be." It was my turn to laugh at him.

Leo stretched his neck and cracked his knuckles. "Hell no. My wolf is dying to go get our mate."

There it was again. The phrase, 'our mate', grated on me. My wolf wanted his own mate, not to share one with my brother. But I also couldn't begrudge my brother his happiness. Not unless Tania chose one of us over the other. Then Leo and I might have words.

We loaded into the truck. It was after dinner and the sun was beginning to set. I glanced at my watch. "It's almost eight. Do you think her gym will still be open?"

Leo grabbed his cell phone, scrolled for a moment, then said. "It closes at nine. Let's go."

We sped down the street, away from the shifter side of town and toward the industrial zone where her gym was housed. The area was mostly inhabited by humans.

The gym had a few parking spots out the front but most were taken. We grabbed the only one available.

I turned off the engine and placed both hands on the steering wheel, my chest tight.

"What's wrong?" Leo asked, having already opened his door to jump out.

I felt like I was paralyzed in the strangest way. "I don't know. It's just..." I stopped, not even sure how I *could* explain the maelstrom of emotions coursing through me.

Did he not feel the same way as me?

Leo chuckled, then whacked me in the chest, startling me. "Come on, man. Things can't get worse."

I wasn't so sure about that. Leo and I had been kind of frozen in place for a long time. Neither of us had committed to any sort of serious relationship. We'd done nothing but save money, working toward freeing our parents. But that hadn't left much time or effort for anything else.

"Mase!" Leo yelled at me, getting out of the car, then thumping the roof. "Let's go."

I forced my stiff limbs out of the truck cabin, then closed the door once more. Back at home, I'd been ready to jump out of my skin to see Tania, but now that we were here, I wasn't sure what to do. Or say. She didn't seem to feel the pull of the fated mate link.

I was as sure as I could be that she was mine, and so was my wolf.

Leo was racing ahead, and I forced myself to follow him up to the large building. He opened the front glass door and went inside.

I took a deep breath, afraid of... I didn't know what. Being rejected by my mate perhaps? But the whole point of the fated mate link was supposedly to make sure that you didn't miss the person when you finally found them, and they couldn't ignore you either.

But Tania wasn't a wolf. What if she *could* ignore it? What if she couldn't feel a fated mate bond like we did? How would we convince her that she was ours?

The glass door closed in front of me as Leo disappeared inside, and panic set in. I refused lose my mate because I was afraid. I'd never backed down from a fight, nor a difficult job. And I certainly wouldn't walk away from the woman that fate had destined would be mine.

My wolf growled inside my chest as if to confirm those thoughts, and I reached out to push open the door. I wasn't about to let my brother win my mate out from under my nose, either.

The air-con hit me in the face, cool air sweeping over my skin. Leo was already chatting with the redheaded woman behind the reception desk, and my instincts were tingling like mad.

I glanced around. Where was she? I could feel her nearby. Tania was definitely here.

Leo called out to me. "Mase. Come over and sign up."

"Sign up?" The words were ringing a bell, but my wolf was way too close to the surface, which meant I couldn't think properly right now.

"Yeah. Come on."

I strode over to the desk and saw the sign-up forms on the counter. They brought me a touch back toward my human side. "Oh yeah. Cool." I signed up to a yearly plan, opened my wallet, and took out enough money for the fee.

The girl behind the desk blinked at me. "You want to pay the whole lot up front? In cash?"

Leo did the same thing, pulling out a chunk of change and placing it down on top of his completed form. "Yeah. We both do."

We always paid cash, had no credit cards, and only took out loans for the houses we renovated.

The woman took our money, shaking her head, but her smile was huge.

Leo caught my eye, then shrugged. They musn't get many paying up front here. The woman typed on the computer for a minute, then handed over two passes. "These are temporary for now, if you wanna head in. We close in just under an hour, but I'll have your permanent cards ready by then. Just grab them on the way out."

"Thanks," Leo said, grinning at the woman, before walking through to the main section of the gym.

When I followed him, I stopped short for a moment. The space was huge, so much bigger than it looked from the outside. Mirrors reached from floor to ceiling, and a custom mural was painted on the large wall facing the mirrors.

There was every type of work-out machine you could imagine, but the gym was definitely skewed toward weight lifting and building. There were only a few treadmills tucked away in a corner, but the weights, tires, ropes and bench-pressing areas were vast.

My wolfy instincts tingled and I turned my head to see Tania standing near her office, her head thrown back in a laugh as she chatted with a huge man, looming over her.

He gave her a shove that knocked her sideways. She stumbled and twisted back to glare at him.

I saw red.

Who the fuck was pushing my mate around?

I charged up to the giant and shoved him in the chest, knocking him back against her office window. "What the hell are you doing pushing Tania like that?"

The man's eyes flared and the purple flash told me he was a supernatural, but not a shifter. This was a warlock.

Tania jumped between us in a flash, her hands out to the huge man and her back to me. "Dad. Stop. It's fine."

"Dad?" I repeated, staring at the giant and suddenly seeing the same dark eyes, the same full lips...

Tania twisted around to look at me, her gaze full of anger. "Mason. What are you doing here?"

I swallowed hard, my anger shrinking just as quickly as it had flared. "I... we joined the gym... and I saw him push you..."

The man behind Tania chuckled. "You don't know my daughter very well, mate, if you think she can't deal with a bit of a shove when she was the one giving me shit."

His accent caught me off guard. He sounded Australian, or at least, something like the Australians I'd heard in TV shows. Not that I was in a position to ask. I'd just shoved the guy. Hard, too.

Leo swaggered up, laughing. "I can see you're making friends already, Mase." He leaned in and held out his hand to Tania's dad. "I'm Leo."

"Jack." The giant shook my brother's hand.

I nodded at him. "I'm Mason."

The giant reached out for me and I shook his hand also, heat flooding up my cheeks. "Sorry about that."

Jack chuckled again, sounding like he was in good humor. "You've got balls, mate, I'll give you that. What do you lift?"

I glanced over at the gym area. "Not sure. This is our first time in the gym. I don't normally work out. Not like this, anyway. Work can be pretty physically demanding, but lift? No idea."

Tania unexpectedly piped up. "Mason and Leo are builders, Dad. They renovate houses."

Jack grunted. "Good to know. Come on." He gestured for us to follow, and headed over to one of the areas that held bench-presses and weights.

I glanced at Tania, who lifted her eyebrows. "What are you waiting for? Go train with him."

"But I came to see you."

She rolled her eyes. "I own the place. I'm not going anywhere. Go train and I'll see you both later."

Tania walked into her office and shut the door.

I glanced at Leo who shrugged and said, "Why not?" And then he headed off to join Jack at the bench press.

I took a deep breath and let it out in a long sigh. We may have found our fated mate, but I had so many questions, and no answers. Once again.

I wasn't sure how long my patience would last, but I gripped onto it with two hands and tried to hold on tight.

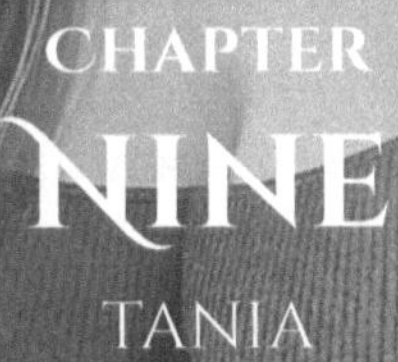

CHAPTER

NINE

TANIA

When Mason had come at my dad, pushing him against the window, all my instincts had fired into action. I'd been ready to take the wolf shifter's head off and demand to know what the hell his problem was.

That was, until I realized that he was trying to defend me. His words still echoed in my ears.

What the hell are you doing pushing her like that?

No-one had ever jumped to my defense before. No-one except my parents, of course. I'd always been the tallest girl around, and the biggest in my class for years. I was the one who'd always defended others. I stood up to the bullies. Not the other way around.

I wasn't sure how I felt about that. It gave me a warm feeling deep inside, but it also kind of unsettled me. I hid in my office for a while after my dad took the boys off to train, my heart pumping wildly and my stomach twisted with anxiety. Mom wasn't here, and I needed her opinion on the guys. She'd already agreed to help me with them, but it would be good to confirm that now.

59

I grabbed my cell phone and sent a text to my all-knowing mother.

Her response was immediate.

On my way.

I chuckled, slid my phone back onto my desk and walked to the door. My breath caught in my throat, and I was embarrassed to admit that I was nervous to open the door and step back into my own gym.

Those two men out there made my whole body tremble with need. I had no idea why I was so intensely attracted to them, nor why they kept giving the impression that they cared about me, but it would all come out in the end.

They needed my help with the spell, and once they got what they wanted, I was pretty sure I'd never see them again.

When I finally opened the door, I gaped at how empty the gym had become.

It wasn't quite closing time yet. What was going on? I narrowed my eyes on a corner of the room and realized everyone was standing in a circle, watching a competition.

I stepped out of my office just as Mom arrived. She rushed over and grabbed onto my arm, like she often did. "What's happening?" she asked.

"I'm not sure," I answered honestly. "I left Dad with the wolf brothers, then went into the office."

Mom stiffened a little as though getting ready for a fight. "They're still here?"

I nodded my head. "Yeah. Come meet them."

We walked, together, over to the training station where everyone was standing around.

As I got closer, I wasn't surprised to see Dad at the center of the excitement. He was standing over the two wolf shifters, who were sweating and grunting as they pushed huge weights in a squat.

"Is that them?" Mom whispered.

I nodded. "Yep."

Dad was counting each squat, encouraging them, yelling at them, mocking them for groaning when he added more weight.

I added up the pounds they were both lifting, quickly estimated their body weights, and was shocked at the result. They'd win almost any lifting competition they competed in, and if their flat abs and bulging biceps were anything to go on, they'd be competitive in a body builder competition, too.

Having both 'go' and 'show' was rare. Very rare. And they both had it.

Mom gasped. "Your dad likes them."

"How do you know?" I whispered.

"Look at his face, his posture. The way he's pushing them. He only does that when he thinks the person has potential. He wouldn't waste his time, otherwise."

Looking back on my own childhood, I had to agree with her.

Sweat poured off Leo and Mason. They were red and hurting, that was for sure.

Leo began to tip to one side and called out. "Jack!"

Dad grabbed the bar with one hand, then raced around behind Leo to ease the bar from his shoulders.

Leo groaned and stepped forward, staggering, then stood straight, a huge smile splitting his face.

Dad clapped him on the back. "Well done."

Mason was still standing, though he shook with strain. He was the older brother, and now that I looked at him, it was obvious. He was slightly larger, the lines around his eyes more defined.

"You done?" Dad asked him.

Mason groaned. "One more."

Dad nodded and got behind him and called out. "Fifty."

Mason went down in a perfect squat and pushed up, his thighs shaking as he grunted out his pain.

The group around us called out and clapped as Dad took the bar from Mason, and the older brother fell forward, Leo catching him in a sweaty hug.

My heart squeezed tight, seeing their comradeship. Being an only child, I'd missed out on a sibling relationship. From what I could tell, it could be strained, and outright violent at times. But the loyalty that ran between these brothers was clearly bone deep. And I was truly envious of people who made a blood bond like that work.

I glanced at my mom, gratitude filling me for the relationship I had with my parents. It was great, and just as rare.

"What do you think, Mom?" I asked. "Will you help me with the spell?"

She turned stared at the boys. "I need to take a closer look at them. I'll let you know in a few minutes."

Mom let go of my hand and walked over to Dad, who was grinning and wiping sweat from his brow.

The spectator group thanked the guys for the entertainment, then headed off to the showers. The gym shut soon, but I had the feeling the wolves wouldn't be leaving straight away.

I grinned at my dad as he walked over to me, watching the wolves still staggering around. "You found some common ground, I see."

Dad chortled. "Yeah. They're pretty raw, but they've got potential."

Mom patted Dad's shoulder. "I'm going to speak to the wolves."

Dad's eyebrows rose as he twigged. "*They're* the wolf shifters you were talking about?"

I nodded. "Yeah. You didn't put it together?"

Dad grunted, crossing his arms over his chest. "Now their strength makes sense. It's not as impressive now that I know they're supernaturals."

I laughed, elbowing my dad in the side. "You wouldn't say that if they were warlocks."

My dad narrowed his eyes. "Wolves have a natural strength. I had to work at it."

I put my hands on my hips. "Dad. You know they just lifted enough to beat anyone in their weight division, with no training. Be fair."

I could have just let it go. Agreed with my dad that being wolves gave them an unfair advantage. But I knew better, and so did he.

Dad glanced away as Mom rushed back to us saying, "Yes! I definitely have to help them."

My jaw dropped. "Seriously?"

She nodded, her eyes wide as though she was surprised. Or scared. "I had decided I wasn't going to help you with them. I had no intention of liking them…"

"But?" I asked her, my heart pumping a little stronger and harder in my chest.

"They're…" Mom stopped to swallow hard. "Important. To you."

It was my turn to open my eyes wide. "What are you talking about?"

Mom wrung her hands together, flicking her gaze from me to Dad, then back again. "I… can't explain it fully. I just know that I need to help them, or at least, help you."

Dad started to ask her something, but she only shook her head and took a step toward the door. "I'm going to find a spell book I've got at home. Can you pop by tomorrow to get it?"

Mom waved at my father to follow. He did, with a massive shrug of his shoulders and a perplexed glance at me.

Leo raced after him, shaking Dad's hand and thanking him for a great session. The frost around Dad's aura melted the moment Leo grinned at him.

Mason stepped up next to me, chugging down a bottle of water. He didn't say anything but he radiated heat, making my skin shiver even though he wasn't even touching me.

"He could sell ice to a snowman," Mason said suddenly, nodding at his younger brother.

I laughed. "Yeah. He certainly seems to have a way with people." I turned to look at Mason, his dark hair falling over his face. I immediately wanted to reach out and brush it back.

Before I could do such a silly affectionate thing, I curled my fingers into my palms and put both hands behind my back. "So… my Mom wants to help with the spell. Looks like you're getting two witches for the price of one."

Mason's gaze softened, then he ran an uncertain hand through his hair. "I still can't believe you're going to help us."

"I'm going to try," I said, and speaking of which, if I was right about the correlation between my physical strength and my magical power, I needed to put in a big work out tonight.

Mason nodded. "That's all we can ask."

Leo swaggered back over to join us, a huge grin on his face. "Your dad is great."

I couldn't help the answering smile on my own lips. "I know."

Leo and Mason stared at me for a little too long, and when the desire swirled without warning in my gut, I took a step toward the front door, thinking it was best they left. "I'm so glad you guys joined the gym. Means I have to hold up my end of the bargain."

The guys followed me to the front door, but they still weren't talking.

I chattered away, filling the intense silence. "Mom wants me to look at a spell book tomorrow with her, then... do you know when you can get your parents to come over so we can try and reverse the curse?"

Leo and Mason glanced at each other.

"Our parents check in with us every day, usually at sunset." Mason glanced outside. "We've probably missed them tonight, but if we told them to be somewhere in a couple of days, at a certain time, they'd come."

I nodded, worrying my bottom lip with my teeth. Mason's gaze dropped to my mouth and held there.

Another hot flush of arousal washed over me, and I glanced away, ashamed at being so easily aroused by two men who would never go for a woman like me. "I'll talk to Mom tomorrow, then we'll set up a place and time to try the spell reversal."

Leo pushed a business card at me. "We wrote our cell numbers on our gym forms, but if you need us, you can get us here."

I took the card and stared down at the simple white card. Two names, two cell numbers and an email. "I'll let you know as soon as Mom and I work out the best way to do this."

"Thank you," Leo whispered, stepped forward and kissed me on the cheek.

The touch of his lips on my skin made me shiver, and an involuntary gasp rose from my throat.

Mason growled and pushed his brother out of the way. The hairs on the back of my neck stood on end and I was frozen in place. Waiting to see what would happen next.

When Mason took my face in his hands, the world shifted on its axis and I knew things were never going to be the same again.

TEN

MASON

My wolf snarled inside my mind when Leo kissed her cheek. Pushing my brother out of the way was the least violent thing I wanted to do to him.

But then I had my hands on my mate, cupping her face and lifting her chin so I could stare down into her beautiful brown eyes. I couldn't look away, and despite my wolf growling his desperate desire to claim her, I stilled. Breathless with awe.

"God, you're beautiful."

Any fire and desire I'd seen in her eyes moments ago, disappeared like it had never been. She practically snarled at me as she stepped back. "You guys can leave. I'll call you tomorrow when I know what's going on."

She marched past the reception desk and opened the glass door, waving at us to exit.

I stared at her, totally shocked. "What did I say?"

Her face hardened and her lips thinned.

She wasn't going to explain, that was obvious.

I stumbled to the door, and she stepped back so I couldn't touch her.

Leo followed closely behind me, ready to smooth the way. "We'll call you tomorrow when we can talk to our parents."

"Tania, I..." I reached out to her, wanting to fix whatever I'd accidentally broken.

She looked away, angry slashes of color in her cheeks.

I glanced at my brother, but he simply shoved me in the side. "Let's go. I stink. So do you. It's time for a shower."

I let my brother move me where I didn't want to go—outside and away from Tania. She slammed the door shut, then locked it with a click.

I tried to catch her gaze, to show her in my expression I was sorry even though I had no idea what I'd done wrong. She spared me a momentary glare before flicking her long dark hair over her shoulder and sauntering away.

"What the hell went wrong there?" I whispered.

Being able to get my hands on my mate after all this time had gone a hell of a lot better in my head than the real thing.

"Come on." Leo walked toward the truck.

I shoved my hands into my pockets and straggled after him. My gut was tight and angry, but there was a deep sense of rejection and hurt that I hadn't experienced before. Probably because none of the women I'd dated in the past had been my mate.

If they'd pulled away from me, or turned me down, I would've taken it in my stride. Not today. Not with Tania.

I was gutted.

I jumped in the passenger side, letting Leo drive us home. I still wasn't sure what went wrong, and although I assumed my brother didn't either, I asked him anyway.

"Hey. Do you know what the fuck just happened?"

Leo's chortle ground down on a raw nerve, and I growled softly to let him know.

"Hey, hey, calm down."

The very last thing you should say to someone when you want them to calm down.

"I was just laughing at the fact that, for the first time ever... you got rejected." Leo chuckled away like it was the funniest thing ever.

Not for the first time today, I wanted to smash him in the face. "I've been knocked back before."

Leo shook his head. "No, you haven't. But anyway, don't stress about that shit. We need to work out why our mate doesn't like being told that she's beautiful."

I twisted around to stare at my brother. "What?"

Leo shrugged. "You told her she was beautiful, and she went from melting wax, to freezing you out. She either doesn't believe you, or she thinks you're just buttering her up so she'll do the spell for us. Either way, we've gotta get our parents sorted, and then we can focus on our mate."

I nodded, staring back at the road. Leo was onto something there. Tania was a larger girl, but in all the right places. Huge ass, strong thighs, big breasts I could lose myself in for days. And I intended to do so in the future.

The problem must be the guys in her past. Those stupid warlocks had probably never given her the attention a goddess like her deserved.

"Hey Leo. How do you feel about sharing a mate with me?"

We pulled into our driveway and Leo shut off the truck's engine.

He turned blue eyes on me, looking wary. "I don't like it. Why?"

It was my turn to laugh. "Then why do you seem so cool with it?"

He sighed. "Because the fated mate bond is never wrong. If we're meant to share a mate, we're meant to share a mate. I'm not going up against fate or leaving Tania to risk never finding a woman again. She's perfect for me, and for you. Or so we've been told. That's what the bond means. Maybe she's the one who needs both of us? I don't know. And yeah, my wolf gets fucking jealous and edgy, but I could never walk away."

I couldn't fault his logic; in fact he made a whole lot of sense.

Leo stared ahead out of the windscreen, then his face lit up. "Hey. They're here."

He jumped out of the vehicle and slammed the door shut behind him.

I looked out to see my parents in their usual wolf form, both waiting patiently near the front entrance of our townhouse.

The sun had set, and it was dark all around. But we'd left the porch light on, and my shifter vision was good. Even in the darkness, I could clearly see the white of my mother's fur coat, and the gray of my father's.

I got out of the truck and followed Leo as he led our parents down the thin alleyway beside our house and around into the backyard.

Leo opened the back door and turned on the outside lights. "I'll get the food." He ducked inside for the raw steak we gave Mom and Dad every night.

I sat down on one of the old deck chairs, wanting to tell all. Mom came up beside me and put her head on my lap. She seemed to somehow feel the heavy weight I had pressing in on me.

I smiled and touched her head, scratching gently behind her ears. Even after all these years, it was still strange to interact with them only as wolves, but it was better than not having them at all.

They had to know how hard we'd been trying to find a way for them to come back to us. "We've found a witch who's going to try and reverse the curse."

Mom's head came up and I could see the startlement in her eyes. Her ears pricked up and I knew that if she was still human, she'd be telling me off for messing with the magicals. That's what had caused all this shit in the first place.

"Don't worry," I told her. "Tania's a good person—the best, actually—and she hasn't promised us anything. She just said she would try her best."

Leo walked outside with two dinner plates for our parents, both containing fresh steak.

He placed their plates down on the low outside table we kept there for Mom and Dad. Our parents took their meals, eating quickly.

I glanced away, then went inside to get myself a beer. I never liked watching them eat for some reason. I think it was because my heart ached to take them inside and have them sit at the table in their human form. I wanted us as a family to share a Sunday roast. Like we used to.

"Want one, Leo?" I held up the beer.

"Yeah. Please."

I popped the tops on two beers and walked back outside, handing my brother his drink while our parents finished eating.

I hated this, more than anything. I wanted to talk to my dad, get his advice. He shouldn't be stuck in a wolf's body. And my mother deserved so much more than running through the forest, dodging poachers, possibly for the rest of her life.

Leo sat forward on his chair. "Tania wants to try to reverse the spell, or at least assess you guys, as soon as possible. Can you hang around here tonight and tomorrow so we can bring her here?"

"You wanna bring her here?" I asked Leo, gesturing to our backyard. "Not exactly the best advertisement of the work we do."

Leo turned to face me. "What do you suggest then?"

We needed a neutral ground, somewhere our parents could easily meet us. "How about in the forest by the river? Isn't that kind of neutral zone for the witches and the shifters?"

Leo glanced back at our parents. "What do you think? Can you meet us there earlier in the evening? Or wait here until we know for sure. I know you guys don't like staying in town during the day, but we have no way of contacting you if Tania needs us."

Dad nodded his huge head and walked up onto the back deck, sitting down on the worn wood.

"That's as good a plan as any. You wanna come inside? Sleep in the lounge?" We'd tried to get our parents to sleep inside, or in a bed before, to no avail.

Mom walked over to Dad and curled against his side. He adjusted his body to curve around her.

Leo chuckled. "They're happy out here. But we could get the bed."

We had a large dog bed, easily big enough to hold two, that we'd bought ages ago and never had the guts to bring them out to show our parents in case they took offence.

Leo went inside and dragged it out, laying it on the porch. It looked like a large gray pillow.

Mom put one paw onto it, then climbed in and curled up with a soft sigh. Dad soon followed, placing his head on her back, and closing his eyes. They didn't look offended at all. They looked comfortable and warm.

I swallowed the lump in my throat that the sight of them together brought up for me. They'd stayed together, and got each other through what had to be the worst ten years of their life.

They were thin, and stressed, and from the looks of them, hadn't felt safe for a long time.

Leo yawned dramatically, then said. "Time for bed, I think. We've got work early in the morning, but we'll let you know about the spell, as soon as we know."

Dad growled a little in acknowledgment, then I went and locked the side gate to give our parents a little extra protection.

"We'll leave the back door unlocked, so if you wanna come in through the night, just come on in."

Mom opened her eyes and nodded, then settled again.

I went inside, shut the door without locking it, and swiped at the errant tear that had fallen on my cheek. *Such a waste...*

Leo was true to his word, and by the time I'd lumbered up the stairs he was already snoring in his bedroom, still dressed and passed out on his bed.

I managed a shower, because working out with Jack had made me sweat like I'd never sweated before.

Then it was time for sleep, but I couldn't stop the dreams that filled my head that night. Dreams of wolves, and magic and kids. Of a future that glowed with a beautiful promise, and yet somehow always seemed just out of reach.

ELEVEN

TANIA

I poured myself a coffee, still shaking my head to try and chase away the tiredness. I'd had the hottest dreams of my life last night. Sex with Leo. Then Mason. Then both of them. At the same time! It had been... insane. And so not me.

I was shocked that even my subconscious mind would entertain such a thing, but since it was just a stupid fantasy, I decided not to chastise myself.

A healthy imagination was good, and a sex drive was normal and healthy too. It had been forever since my last boyfriend, but still... that was probably why my brain was using my dreams to torture me.

I drank my coffee, enjoying the caffeine hit, then my cell phone buzzed in front of me. It was Mom.

Found the book. Can you come over today and we'll go over the spell?

I checked the roster and realized that, for once, I hadn't scheduled myself on.

Sure. Be there in an hour.

After all, what else did I have to do today except figure out how to break a curse on a pair of wolf shifters?

I checked on Mel, who was at the front desk, said hello to some of my regulars, and headed out the door. Mom and Dad's new place was easy walking distance from mine, so I took my time and strolled over there.

The sun was shining, and it was a beautiful day. The heat warmed my face, and for some reason, I wanted to just enjoy *being* today. My mind drifted to Harry, and the life that had ended far too early for my dear friend.

Tears burned my eyes and I shook my head. No. Harry had been an awesome friend, and I should be honoring him with happy thoughts, not wallowing in my grief all the time.

I wasn't sure how easy that would be, since every time I thought about him, all I could focus on was the sadness and waste of his untimely death.

When I reached my parents' place, I laughed when I saw that most of the house siding had already been pulled off. The poor house looked completely undressed, but I knew it wouldn't be long before their work began to pay off. My parents were nothing if not determined to succeed at whatever project they started.

I jogged up to the front door and knocked. "It's open!" Mom's voice came from inside the house.

I pushed open the door, with no idea what sort of disaster zone I'd be walking into. But I was pleasantly surprised to see that most of the inside sported new drywall, and the staircase had been stripped down ready for staining or painting.

"In here," Mom called, and I turned to my right, following the voice.

Another laugh bubbled up when I entered the front sitting room. "Couldn't live in a construction zone too long, Mom?"

The room was completely done—thanks to her magic. There

was no way a contractor could have finished the room so quickly or so perfectly. The walls were a rich green, and the furnishings were antique but dressed in spectacular gold and silver embroidered fabrics. It was both grand, and homely, all in one.

"Gotta have one room done completely," Mom said, looking up from her book. "The rest of the house is still a mess, though."

The back wall was all bookcases filled to the brim. "This is beautiful, Mom."

She smiled at me. "I love being surrounded by my books. Some magical, of course. Others literary. Romance. Adventure. Everything. You know me."

I definitely got my love of books from my mom.

She called me closer with a wave of her hand. "Come look at this spell. The one you found is good, but I think this one might be useful to assess the wolves first. See if we can simply lift the curse in a more gentle manner, rather than force it."

I inclined my head over the pretty oak desk at which she was seated, and stared down at the spell. The incantation was complex, like most of the spells my mom liked. But if it worked, it would definitely save the wolves from extra stress.

"I'll bow to your knowledge on this one. Looks like a great spell to try."

Mom stared at me, her lips curled down at the edges. "It's a powerful spell, sweetheart. Would you like me to ask Aunt Maggie to help us?"

Aunt Maggie was Mom's sister. A classic skinny bitch, but a powerful witch.

We didn't get along.

I shook my head. "No, Mom. I've been working on my spells and have improved quite a lot." Understatement of the century. "I can handle this with your help."

In fact, I was pretty sure, with my newfound power, I could

handle it alone, but since Mom wanted to help, I was going to let her. She had a lot more experience than me.

Mom's eyes widened. "Tania, I know you think you can do this spell, but..."

I rolled my eyes. "Test me if you don't believe me. Give me a spell to do, Mom. A hard one."

Her jaw dropped. "You're serious?"

I nodded. I knew she worried about me not having enough magic. She was hesitating because she didn't believe me about being strong. Then I remembered the necklace. "Oh! I made something for you the other day. Let me bring it here."

I closed my eyes and envisioned where I'd hidden the necklace, in a drawer in my dresser. Then I pushed my magic to transport the heavy necklace into my hands.

It was so effortless, fear rippled through me that I'd failed. Just as Mom had expected.

When I opened my eyes, I stared down at my hands. My mom's gold necklace glistened in my palms. "Wow. It worked. I'm still getting used to this feeling."

Mom gaped at me. "What feeling?"

I grinned at her. "Magic being easy."

Mom reached out her hand, slowly. When she touched the necklace I'd made for her, she jumped. "Whoa. It's real."

A laugh bubbled up in my throat. "Yeah, it is. I wanted to test myself the other day, and metalsmithing was always my biggest weakness at school. So here you go. I made this for you."

Like a kid at kindergarten, I handed over the necklace I'd made. But instead of being made with macaroni, the jewel I'd set in the gold for my mom was a large emerald. She took it with tears in her eyes. "Tania... How?"

Should I tell her about Harry? About the genie spell that he'd succeeded in achieving but had died as a result?

Emotions tightened my chest and I wasn't sure I could do it. I shrugged. "It's a long story."

Mom gave me the side eye, then shook her head with a sigh. "Okay. I'll leave that mystery alone for now. I can see your reluctance to share."

But she wouldn't leave it alone forever. I knew my mom.

"Okay. So, should I call the guys? Set up a time to do the spell on their parents?"

Mom nodded and I pulled my cell phone out. Leo's business card had been burning a hole in my back pocket since he gave it to me.

I turned to the window and typed in his number, unable to sit down and relax. My whole body was pulsing with a nervous energy I wasn't sure what to do with.

"H'lo?" Leo's happy voice came barreling through the phone.

"Hey, Leo, it's Tania. The gym owner." Oh my God, I sounded like an idiot.

"Tania! The witch who's gonna save our family. How you doin'?"

I giggled, then rolled my eyes, annoyed that this man turned me into some sort of stupid teenage girl. "We're good. I'm at my mom's new place and we were wondering when we could meet your parents."

It was weird to think that Leo and Mason's parents were wolves, but I was going to be face to face with them soon enough, so I needed to wrap my head around the idea pretty fast.

"Mase and I are at work at the moment, but we asked our parents to stay at our place all day today, so we'd be ready to meet you whenever you called."

"Oh great. Well, how do you want to do this?" I asked.

"We're just in the middle of tiling a bathroom, but if you can come to meet us around one p.m., would that suit?"

I glanced at my mom, who was listening in and nodding. "Yeah, we can do that. You want us to come to your place?"

Leo chuckled. "Well, not really. Our place is a dump. We put all our energy and money into our business, so we don't really want you seeing our townhouse. It's not a good advertisement for our work, or who we are or anything. So please, don't judge us by that."

A flush of heat bloomed in my cheeks. He was worried about what I would think about him and Mason's home? Really?

"Don't be silly," I said. "I'm there to help, no other reason."

"Great! We were thinking we could meet in the forest, at a neutral spot, but it's not really safe for them to roam during the day. If you're okay with coming to our place, despite the mess..."

"I am," I said firmly, wanting to reassure him.

"Okay, Then they'll be in the back yard."

"It's no issue. Text me the address and we'll see you there at one."

"Great. Thanks heaps," Leo said, then he hung up.

I smiled at the happiness in his voice. He was sunshine while Mason felt like... a storm. A fiery storm at that. I tried not to think about the fact he'd almost kissed me last night, even though I was pretty sure the topic would come up when I saw him again.

I had no idea how I was going to handle that.

"What's happening with you and the wolves?"

I turned to look at Mom, her question surprising me. "Me and the wolves? What do you mean?"

She nodded. "Yes. Your energy changes when you speak with either of them. And in the gym they both looked at you like they were going to devour you. And not in a food kind of way."

The heat blossomed into a full-blown furnace in my cheeks. "Oh, don't be silly, Mom."

She stepped forward and gripped my hand. "I'm not being

silly. They both want you, Tania. And I know you can't even imagine..."

I was already stepping out of her touching zone and going back to the spell book. "Mom. Men like that don't date women like me."

"You mean wolf shifters don't date witches?"

This time I glared at her, which I didn't like to do with my mom, but I couldn't help it. "You know what I mean."

"No, I don't, Tania." She snapped back at me. "You're a hardworking, intelligent business owner. You're young. You're beautiful. You're a catch!"

I groaned and dropped my head, staring at the magic book. "You're my mom, so you have to say those things."

I could feel the intensity of her gaze on me and didn't want to lift my head and deal with it. Mom loved Dad's large size, and she transferred that love to me and my curves. But for most of my life I'd been called fat by men and women alike, rejected by boyfriends for my size, and refused jobs by employers who didn't want to hire the big girl.

There was nothing my mom could say that was going to make me think that two sexy, muscular wolf shifters would ever want a woman like me. Not for a date, or anything like that. For my magic? Yeah... I could imagine that. But nothing else.

Happily, Dad walked into the room at that point and distracted her attention when he started talking about food.

With my parents both distracted, I sat down on Mom's plush new couch with the magic book and went over the spell we were about to cast.

CHAPTER

TWELVE

LEO

"Come on, man! We've gotta go!"

Ever since I told Mason that we had to meet Tania at our place at one p.m., he'd been dragging his feet. Why he'd do that when we were so close to our goal, I didn't know.

Now, he'd finally put his tools down and was washing his hands like a germophobe. Which he was not. The man didn't shower every day, and as a wolf, he drank out of dirty puddles.

This was getting ridiculous. I checked my watch for the hundredth time, running a frazzled hand through my hair. "Seriously, Mase. I'm going to leave without you."

I grabbed my keys out of my back pocket and turned away from him. What did I actually need him for anyway? We'd paid for the gym membership already, so technically our debt with Tania was done.

The way he was acting it was probably best I went alone anyway. Tania was... touchy. And Mason seemed to know exactly which button to push to make her mad. Probably best to avoid that today, if possible.

When I reached the truck, I didn't hesitate or check to see if my brother was hard on my heels. I just pulled open the door and jumped in. Moments later, Mason hopped in the passenger side, breathing hard. I had to assume he'd run after me.

"Finally pulled your finger out?" I asked, turning the key in the ignition and throwing the truck into gear.

Mason threw me a dirty glare, then focused on the road as I whipped through the side streets, racing to get home before Tania arrived.

Mase gasped once, grabbing the door handle at one point when I took a corner too quickly, but he didn't say anything. He knew I hated being late, and being late for our mate? Grrr... I could have punched the idiot in the head.

Despite my haste, she got there before us. A fancy black car was parked out the front of our place and Tania was standing in the front yard, staring up at the old townhouse we called home.

I parked on the street and jumped out, racing for the woman who was about to make our dreams come true. "I am so sorry we're late. Work was... crazy."

She turned and gave me a beautiful smile. "No problem. We just got here."

An older woman stepped down off the porch, smiling politely.

"Oh, hi." I called out to her. "I didn't even see you there."

Tania's mom, Sue, looked nothing like her daughter. She was blonde and petite, and just, not Tania.

Sue grinned at me. "I'm itching to get inside and see if I can do some renovations for you guys."

My jaw dropped. "You wanna renovate our house?"

Tania laughed nervously. "Mom's just over zealous."

"No. I'm serious," she said. "Let me in."

Mason had joined us now and he was the one who said, "Yes ma'am," before walking up to the front door and letting her in.

I could hear her asking questions and Mase answering, in clipped single syllables.

Tania sighed and shook her head. "I can't believe she's in there renovating. Seriously, she has no shame."

I glanced through the front door, seeing a sparkle and a flash of silver light. "What's she doing in there?"

Tania shrugged. "I have no idea. You might wanna go in there and see."

I turned back and stared straight at Tania. "I'm exactly where I wanna be. She can do whatever she wants in there."

Tania's eyes shimmered as though she was going to cry, but there were no tears. There was something else, an emotion I hadn't seen before, and I wasn't sure how to approach her about it.

"Are your parents around the back? Let's go," she said, twisting away and breaking our eye contact. "I want to meet your parents."

She began walking down the sideway and I chased after her. She was wearing black sports tights like she usually did and I couldn't help the way my gaze immediately fell to her luscious ass.

I couldn't wait for the day when I could touch her whenever I wanted to. It was already so difficult not to reach out and grab her.

Tania waited at the gate while I unlocked it and pushed the door open for her. She walked through, then stopped.

I stepped up beside her and closed the gate, only to turn around and see her seemingly frozen in place. "What's wrong?" I asked, glancing over to the back porch where my parents stood, staring at Tania.

Her throat worked as she swallowed hard, then she steepled her fingers together and pressed her nails against her lips. "I've never seen a wolf shifter like this before."

"Never?" I asked, surprised. Though it wasn't super common, there were definitely plenty of us around and most supernaturals had seen a shifter or two in wolf form.

When she shook her head, I laughed to try and break some of the tension. "Well, before we met George that night, I'd never met a warlock before. So there's a first time for everything, isn't there? Let me introduce you."

I held out my hand for her to take, and she grabbed onto me faster than I'd expected. She was shaking a little, which I had to assume was a touch of fear along with her nerves.

"The larger wolf is obviously my father, Patrick." I gestured to where my dad stood on the porch, and he inclined his head.

Tania squeezed my hand even tighter as I dragged her closer to the porch. "It's okay. They're fully aware in wolf form. They're not wild animals. They won't hurt you, I promise. They know you're here to try and help them."

She nodded and shuffled closer. I glanced at my parents, whose keen eyes were moving from Tania to me, and back again.

"My mom's name is Ariel," I told her, grinning at the way she blinked at me. "Yeah, I know it's unusual."

The back door opened and Mason came out, shaking his head.

"What happened?" I called out to him.

His chin came up and his eyes locked onto us. He saw the way we held hands, and the way she pressed into me. And the look of hurt that crossed his expression was enough to make me want to step away from Tania to appease my brother's pain.

But I didn't. She needed me. So instead, I pulled her a little closer. Mason didn't want to share Tania with me, and the only way he was going to get comfortable with this arrangement was when he realized he couldn't live without her.

I kept the subject neutral. "What did she do in there?"

Mase shoved his hands into his pockets and shrugged. "Everything. It's more than we could do in a month with a whole team of guys."

I laughed aloud. "Maybe it was good that we saved all that money. What's your fee, Sue?"

Tania's mom had followed Mason out, and at my question she stuck her nose in the air. "I don't charge for my magic. It's a gift from the gods, to be shared around."

She seemed offended, so I put my hand on my heart and bowed my head. "I didn't mean to offend you. All the witches we've ever met, charge for their services, which we always found to be fair. It is a skill that you've worked hard to achieve, just as we've done with our laboring skills."

When I glanced up, Sue's eyes were sad and reflected understanding. "I'm sorry this has happened to your family. Would you introduce me to your parents?"

"Of course." I reluctantly let go of Tania's hand and moved over to where Sue was standing next to Mom and Dad.

I repeated the introductions, and Sue bent down and shook my parents' paws, showing respect for the people they actually were.

Then Sue moved over to stand beside Tania, and I joined Mason on the porch. My brother was like stone. Unmoving and hard as rock.

I elbowed him in the ribs, just to give him shit. "You need to get your head in the game, brother. We're about to get our parents back."

Sue and Tania were going through a large book that they'd pulled from goodness knows where.

Mason glanced at me. "You're right." He relaxed his shoulders a little, but I knew his biggest concern was the fact that moments ago I'd been holding hands with Tania. And he hadn't been.

Strange how priorities could change so rapidly.

I nudged him again. "And besides, if Tania chooses us both, you'll be seeing me do a lot more than just hold her hand."

The glare I copped from my brother was epic. Award winning.

It would have cowed a lesser man.

I laughed. And clapped him on the back. "Let's do this." I jogged down the stairs and up to the women. "Do you need anything?"

Sue turned to me. "We're going to do a spell to see if we can simply lift the curse, and if that doesn't work, we're going to... Encourage it."

I nodded, not understanding at all. "So, what should we do?"

Tania smiled at me and glanced over my shoulder at my parents. "Could your mom and dad walk over here and stand in front of us? You and Mason should probably stand on the porch, out of harm's way."

I didn't really like the sound of that. It implied that my parents, as well as Sue and Tania, would be the ones *in* harm's way.

But as my parents butted me with their heads and then walked over to Tania, I did as I was told and stayed with my brother on the porch.

Mason was a statue once more, but this time I could tell he was anxious over our parents.

"What did Tania say they were going to do?" he asked.

I frowned at him. "You didn't hear her?" Our wolf shifter hearing was enhanced well above the normal human range.

Mason grunted. "I did. But it didn't make sense."

I chuckled, standing shoulder to shoulder with my brother,

my gut tight in a knot. "You know as much as I do, Mase. Let's watch and pray."

He nodded and we stared at the pair of witches who'd created a lectern to place the book upon and were beginning to chant.

Tania and Sue were saying the same words, silver light whirling around the wolf versions of my parents.

Then the words stopped, the silver light faded, and Sue heaved a sigh. "The witch is still alive. Unfortunately, we can't just lift it off."

Mom and Dad continued to stand in front of the witches, unmoving.

Tania smiled apologetically and walked around our parents, then rushed up to the porch. "We have to use a stronger spell and force the curse to lift. Do you two have any idea why this was done to your parents?"

I glanced at Mason, whose lips turned down.

"We have theories, but no concrete evidence," I explained. "Mom and Dad liked to run in a part of the woods we were told not to go to. It was said that the area was a witch's sacred space. But there was a creek, and it was quiet and... Mom always said we were conceived out there next to the creek." Not a piece of information I often shared with people, but if it was important, then it needed to be said.

Tania nodded, worrying her lip with her teeth. "Let me talk to Mom and we'll see what we can do next."

She rushed back to her mother and I took a few steps back and fell into the porch swing. It creaked a complaint, but held fast.

After so much time, and hope, would we fall at the final hurdle?

THIRTEEN

TANIA

I walked back to Mom, confused. I didn't know of any sacred witch spots in the woods. "Hey Mom. Leo said his parents used to go somewhere in the forest they were told not to. A special place that was sacred for a witch. Any idea where that may be?"

Mom furrowed her brow. "The forest? You mean…" She gasped suddenly. "Oh no. I think I know what they're talking about, and if I'm right, it means trouble."

Mom turned to the wolves. "Did you go near the cabin at the base of the hills?"

Ariel nodded her head.

"Shit." Mom pressed her fist against her mouth and turned away to stare at the fence.

I glanced over at the boys who were still standing on the porch. I shrugged to show them I had no idea what was going on, then reached out for Mom's arm. "What am I not getting here?"

She turned back to me, her eyes wide and concerned. "The

witch in the woods. She's an ancient. If *she* cursed these wolves, I don't have enough magic to lift such a spell."

Resolution tightened in my gut. "Will we be punished if we lift it?"

Mom stared at me, then slowly shook her head. "I don't think so. But she is an ancient, and her rules are to be obeyed."

My mother had never taught me such a thing before, and frustration clawed at me. "Mom. These poor people have been wolves for over fifteen years. Their sons were left to be raised by outsiders. There is no way they did anything terrible enough to warrant such a curse, and whatever they did, they've done their time. I'm sure they're sorry for trespassing on the witch's special place."

I was all for paying my dues, but the punishment had to fit the crime.

My mom still wasn't moving. Instead her eyes were filling with tears. "I can't."

I grabbed the hair tie from around my wrist and pulled my hair up into a messy bun on top of my head. In some ways it felt like I was preparing for a battle. "Well, I can. As long as you're sure we won't be punished, I'll do the spell anyway."

It was obvious my mom was paralyzed by some fear that had been instilled in her when she was young. My grandparents had been strict and had used some powerful spells to keep her in line. Because of that, I'd been raised with probably too much love and freedom, not that I was complaining.

Mom wrapped her arms around her body. "You aren't strong enough to do the spell on your own."

"Once again, Mom. I can. Remember the necklace? Just tell me it's okay to try."

She nodded. "You can try."

I twisted and gestured to the guys. "Leo, come grab Mom for me."

The gorgeous man rushed over and put a gentle arm around my mother and guided her back to the porch. He didn't ask why, he just helped. Because I asked for it.

Thank you, Leo, I thought. Then, *poor Mom.*

I shook myself, pushing aside my worry for my mother. I had to focus. The book Mom had brought with her had some good spells, but the one I'd found was the one I wanted to try.

I closed Mom's book and magicked up the one from my room. I'd placed it on the couch, in my spot, so I'd know exactly where it was if I needed to call it here.

The lectern was large enough for both books, so I placed mine on top of Mom's, feeling the vibration of age-old magic at my fingertips.

I stopped and took a breath, giving thanks for the powers I'd been given. By my parents, by my teachers, and most recently, by Harry and his genie gift.

It felt natural and right to place my hands on the book, so I gripped the edges of the pages and began to read. The words were written in an ancient language I didn't quite understand, but the message was clear.

I was forcing the curse from the wolves, and giving them back their lives.

The spell had to be recited four times. I finished the first round, and a gust of magic pushed the wolves to the ground, pressing them down into the dirt.

They didn't fight the magic, but their whimpers of distress caught at my heart.

I knew the boys and Mom would be worried, but I couldn't think of them just yet.

The spell. Only the spell.

I began the second recitation, sweat rolling down the sides of my face and my cheeks blooming with heat. I focused on the words, on saying every single syllable correctly.

When I lifted my gaze to look at the wolves, a cloud of mist had descended on them. They were still there, I was sure, but they weren't visible anymore. Not even a hair, or the tip of an ear, poked out of the mist.

I heard my name being called, in what sounded like a shout of panic.

I blocked the noises out and began the third reading. This time there was pain, in my body and quite obviously in theirs from the sound of the howls emerging from the mist. The wolves' distress bit into my resolve and my knees began to shake from the strain.

The curse was pushing me down, making my spine ache and my muscles cramp. It wanted to stay; it didn't want me to win.

I forced my gaze up, to where Leo and Mason were straining forward on the porch, their faces stricken with fear.

Those men deserved their parents back.

Their parents deserved their lives back.

Tears burned in my eyes as I gripped the edges of the book and held on tight as I finished the third reading.

There was only one more round to do. The mist had become silver and sparkling, and I could feel the curse in the air. It would need somewhere to be channeled. Somewhere solid and secure.

We hadn't thought of that, and hadn't brought anything for the purpose.

I let go of the book and pulled my grandmother's gold ring off my finger. My dad's mom. My Nanny. She'd loved me, and I'd loved her, and that bond forged the jewelry in my hand.

It was the last thing my grandmother ever made for me, and I was certain it would be strong enough to hold the curse.

Tears streamed down my cheeks as I placed the ring on the book in front of me, held onto the lectern and began the final reading.

The words flowed from my tongue. My eyes were too blurred from tears to read from the pages anymore, so I recited on memory alone.

There was a large crack, and a human scream. I didn't stop. The words were almost done, and the pain in my back was intense. I gasped out against it.

It wasn't real. The flames on my back were only magic, designed to stop me from finishing the spell. But fuck...they hurt. They *burned*.

I cried out as I went down to my knees, clinging to the lectern. There were only two sentences left and I pushed them out. Every word. And then the spell was done. Complete.

Then everything went black.

Mason

I LEAPED from the porch the moment the spell was done. Tania was on her knees, barely conscious and I needed to get to her before...

Too late. She hit the grass just as I reached her.

I rolled her onto her back, checking for vital signs. I put my head to her chest and heard the steady and rapid thump of her heart beneath her ribs.

Her chest was rising and falling, so she was still breathing. But she seemed to be asleep. Or passed out.

Sue knelt down next to her daughter on the grass, running her hands over Tania's face and through her hair. "She's okay." There was relief in her tone. "She'll wake up soon."

Tania's eyelids fluttered and her head began to turn from side to side. "What happened?"

"You fainted," I said, putting my arm around her to help as she tried to sit up.

"Seriously?" She frowned as though she didn't believe me.

Then she squinted up into the air. "Who's that?"

I turned to stare in the direction she was looking and saw someone I didn't recognize. I jumped to my feet; my hands clenched into tight fists. Why was there a man, and a naked man at that, standing in our backyard?

Leo rushed over to the dirty, scraggly man, his eyes shining with tears. "Dad?"

I gulped as the man turned toward Leo and embraced him.

On the ground sat an older woman, staring at her hands as she moved them in front of her face. "Mom?" My voice came out squeaky with shock.

She rose to her feet, awkward and clumsy, like a newborn giraffe.

"Clothes," Sue said from behind me, clicked her fingers, and covered my parents with simple cotton clothing.

I turned to smile my relief at her, and she shrugged. "I know wolves don't care about nudity, but... still."

"Thanks," I managed to choke out as I staggered over to where my mom stood, staring at me.

"Mom." I opened my arms and she stepped into my embrace, hugging me as tightly as I held her.

My heart burst with joy, and at the same time grew larger and stronger. "I can't believe it's really you." I pulled back to cup her face. Her skin was scratchy and dirty, her hair tangled and pulled over her face.

I turned to Tania, not letting go of my mother. "Thank you. From the bottom of my heart, thank you."

Tania smiled at me through her tears.

Then I turned back to Mom, frowning. "They're not speaking." I threw another glance Tania's way. "Is that... normal after such a spell?"

Tania wiped at the tears on her cheeks. "They haven't spoken as a human in over a decade. I expect they need a few minutes to work everything out again."

Oh. True.

Leo came over to cuddle Mom and I raced over to give Dad a hug, before walking back to Tania. "I don't know how to thank you," I said again. "You've just given us back everything."

"Your joy is enough," she said, her tone full of emotion.

I glanced at Sue. "And what you did to our house is... beautiful. Thank you." None of what she had done was particularly to my taste, but she'd increased the value of our property by at least a hundred thousand dollars, and saved us many hours of back-breaking work. Thank you wasn't enough.

Sue grinned at me. "I did it for your parents."

I frowned at her. "You..." Then it hit me, and I laughed. "You made this house to *their* taste so they can live here."

She laughed. "Yes. Well... I guessed at their style. But they're my age, and haven't lived in a home for a long time so I went with lush, but comfortable."

"You have impeccable taste," I said, her care touching my heart. "I really don't know how to thank you. Either of you. Words are not enough."

And they weren't. In fact, they were vastly inadequate.

"I assume you have another home you can move into when it's time?" Sue asked.

I nodded. "We bought another house this week actually. The plan was to flip it, but it would easily do to live in."

She clapped. "Great. Well, we better be going. I'm sure you four have lots to catch up on."

Tania smiled at me and turned to go.

I reached out for her, unable to let her go without thanking her properly. "Tania. Please."

She put her hand over my fingers and smiled at me. "You don't owe me anything, Mason. Seriously. I'm just so grateful I could help you get your family back."

"Can I do something for you?" I asked. "Do you have a home that needs renovating the old-fashioned way? Or perhaps you want more business? There's lots of shifters who would pay well for a witch as fearless, and powerful, as you."

Tania opened her mouth to respond, but Sue grabbed her daughter and grinned at me. "You should definitely find my beautiful daughter more people to help, and if I decide to buy some more property in the area, you'll be my first call."

I smiled at Sue and squeezed Tania's arm, loving the feel of her warm skin beneath my fingers. "You did so well. You were amazing. I... thank you."

I sounded like an idiot, saying the same thing over and over, and I expected to be told so.

But instead, Tania stepped close and wrapped her arms around me, holding me tight.

I closed my eyes and slid my hands to her back, marveling at how perfect it felt to have my mate against my body. She pressed her lips to my ear and said, "You deserve to be happy."

Then she kissed my cheek and my wolf whimpered inside my chest. She was going to leave. I couldn't let her go.

She pulled away and I grabbed for her. "No."

She smiled. "It's okay. You know where to find me if you want to talk."

I nodded as she pulled away this time. "Yes. But..."

Sue stepped up and tucked her hand into her daughter's elbow. "Don't worry Mason. You'll be seeing us in the future. But I need to take my daughter home. She's had a big day."

"Mom." Tania rolled her eyes as though her mom was being overprotective, but I suddenly noticed the pallor in Tania's cheeks.

Despite my wolf desperately aching to wrap my mate up in his arms, I had to let her go. Her mother needed to care for her, in whatever special magic ways they had.

And one day soon, hopefully, I'd be the one to look after her when she wasn't well.

"Okay," I said, and reluctantly watched my mate walk away.

CHAPTER

FOURTEEN

MASON

The howl in my heart echoed in my head. But one look back from Sue, over her shoulder as she and Tania walked away, and my wolf quietened down.

My father reached out a hand and squeezed my shoulder and I turned toward him. His hair was thin, and he was balding. But he was still as tall as I remembered, with a strong face and the kind eyes I recognized whether in human or wolf form.

"Dad."

He opened his arms and I stepped close, embracing his thin frame properly this time. It would take time to get him and Mom back to good health, but I would devote all my resources to make sure my parents never suffered again.

"Welcome home." I directed them to follow me inside the newly renovated house.

"What do you mean?" Mom asked, walking closely behind me. Her voice sounded faintly scratchy, as if she was still getting used to using it.

I opened the back door and led them into the kitchen and

open plan living area. "I mean… Sue used her magic to renovate this whole place, especially for you two. We bought another house earlier this week and can move in straight away. This place is for you. And the mortgage is paid off." Or it would be once we finished our current job.

Mom walked over to the island countertop, running a hand over the expensive marble. "No. Mason, we can't do that."

Her voice was soft, broken almost. Rusty.

I glanced at Leo, who was staring with big eyes at our transformed kitchen. Before, there had been cracks in the drywall, olive green lino on the floors, and purple cabinetry that made the ultimate eighties statement.

We hadn't been worried about living in a place that should have been gutted to the studs or torn down. It had been a means to an end.

Now it was a palace. A palace fit for our parents.

Leo put his arm around our mother's frail shoulders. "Welcome home, Mom. Let's take you guys on a proper tour and look at what else Sue did for you."

Leo headed off with Mom, and I went to the fridge, newly stocked with food and drinks. "Dad, want a beer?"

Dad chuckled, the sound rusty and strained. "Love one. God, I can't believe this isn't a dream. I'm actually here, with you. As a human."

I pulled out three beers and a lasagna dish, another magical gift from Tania's mother. "You hungry?"

Dad's eyes went big and round. "Famished." Then he licked his lips. "I feel like I haven't eaten in years."

"You haven't. Not like this." I slid the pasta dish into the new, stainless-steel oven and pushed the beer over to my dad. "Drink Dad. Rest. Shower. Sleep. Whatever you want. The nightmare is finally over."

He sat on the new barstool, then put his head in his hands. "God... a shower. Yes... that's definitely first on my list. After this beer."

There were so many things I wanted to say to him, so many questions I wanted answered. But it all came down to one thing. "I've missed you, Dad."

He stared at me, then nodded. "I've missed you too. You and Leo. Your mom and I... we missed so much."

I gulped down my beer, afraid I'd cry at any moment. "Well, you're just in time to meet my mate."

Dad took a sip of the beer, then grimaced at the flavor. "That's different than I remember." Then he looked up at me and blinked. "What did you say?"

I grinned at him, and pulled out a stool for myself. I dragged it around the island to sit so I was still close to the oven and the fridge. "Tania. The witch who broke the spell for us. She's my fated mate."

My dad's grin split his face. "Son. I'm so happy for you."

I put my hand up to stop him from moving as he looked ready to jump up and hug me. Maybe even offer further congratulations, when I really wasn't sure it was warranted.

"What's wrong?" he asked, his grin fading.

"She's a witch for one thing, Dad. Not what I'd expected, at all."

He shrugged. "She's beautiful, and powerful. And obviously with a good heart, if she helped our family without requiring payment. There's no rule that says your mate has to be a wolf shifter, too."

"True." There was no rule, but it was generally frowned upon to marry outside the pack.

"There's something else," I said, getting to the heart of the issue. It was this part that had me most concerned.

"Tell me." His lips thinned as he readied himself for the bad news.

I lifted my beer and took a swig of the cold hops, enjoying the way it washed down my throat. I steeled myself to say the words I dreaded. "She's... ah, Leo's mate too. Or so he says."

I waited for the sky to fall. For my dad's shock and anger to rear its ugly head. But instead, his eyes lit up with a happiness I'd never seen before, then he burst out laughing.

"Dad!"

He slapped his hand on the table, chuckling away. "Well, she's one lucky girl, isn't she?"

I pinched the bridge of my nose. "Dad, it's not funny. How am I meant to share my woman... with my *brother*?"

Dad took another swig of beer, grimacing a little less this time. "Son. A fated mate is the biggest blessing of anyone's life. Don't let your insecurities get in the way of your happiness. Trust me, I know. I used to worry about so many things. Money. Providing for my family. So many petty little things, that in the end meant nothing. I missed seeing you and Leo grow up and become men, and I'd do anything to get that time back."

"It wasn't your fault, Dad."

He smiled sadly, "I know that... in a way. But my point is, there's only one thing worth living for... hell, only one thing worth dying for, and that's your woman. If she's big enough, powerful enough... hell, *strong* enough to take on both my sons, then she deserves you."

I took another drink and sighed. "She hasn't chosen us yet."

That was when my father grew serious, the intensity in his eyes leveling me. "Then it's up to you, Son, isn't it? Don't you dare let her get away."

Tania

I BRUSHED Mom's arm away from my shoulders and collapsed onto my couch. She was hovering like a bloody fly. "I'm fine, Mom. Seriously. You can stop."

"Oh hush. You look like death warmed up."

Mom used her magic to make me a cappuccino and a platter of danishes appeared on the coffee table in front of me.

"Eat," she proclaimed, sitting on the couch next to me. "I've put some healing magic on both."

I sighed but reached for the coffee and took a sip. A warmth flooded me that I remembered from my childhood. I laughed and looked up at her. "That's familiar."

She shrugged, "So sue me. I didn't like it when you hurt yourself, even if you did enjoy throwing yourself around like your father."

I ate one of the pastries, then settled back onto the couch. "I'm still feeling exhausted, but better. Thanks Mom."

Her eyes shimmered with unshed tears. "I'm so sorry, Tania."

I sat up, frowning. "Sorry? What for?"

"For pulling back, for failing you. You needed me to help you with that spell, and I..."

I grabbed both of her hands. "Mom. You did not disappoint me. I was actually proud of myself for doing that spell without your help."

In fact, I was rapt that I'd been able to do the spell alone. It had proven to everyone—myself included—that I was indeed, now wielding powerful magic.

Mom wiped at the tears that had splashed onto her cheeks. "I am immensely proud of you, sweetheart. That spell would have knocked most witches on their asses."

A laugh bubbled up out of my throat. "Thanks." Though the fact that I'd passed out was a little concerning.

She patted my leg. "Keep eating. You'll feel better, the more you have. Then you need a sleep."

I glanced at the clock. It was after two. "I need to get down to the gym. My shift starts soon."

Mom stood up and shook her head at me. "No way. I'll speak to Jaydy downstairs."

My mom knew Jaydy, of course, as we'd been besties for so long.

I shook my head. "No, she's been working since six this morning..."

"Tania Joy Masterson. Listen to me." Mom put her hands on her hips and glared down at me. "I will sort this out."

I opened my mouth to rebut her, but she said, "Tania, please. I've been no use today at all... and... please. Let me do this one thing."

I didn't let anyone take over my business. I'd lived and breathed the gym since the day of its inception. I managed it, owned it, worked it almost every day. But looking into my mother's eyes, I had to push past my fear of letting go of the reins.

After all, if I couldn't trust my mother, who could I trust?

I let out a loud sigh. "Okay, Mom."

"You have a nap." She took backward steps toward the hatch that led back down to the gym. Then she raised her hand and snapped her fingers and I was lying on my bed.

I laughed and yelpedat the same time. Then I called out, "Tracey should be available. Or Anne. Maybe. But Jaydy needs a break."

"Sleep!"

I lay my head on my pillow and chuckled. There was no arguing with her, and if I was really honest, I felt like utter trash.

I closed my eyes and let myself relax, my mind going straight to Leo and Mason. Such an amazing pair of brothers. Like night and day. Light and dark. Funny and serious. Sexy and cute. But both good people.

Good brothers. Good workers. Good sons.

Good lovers...

"Oh, shut up and go to sleep." I groaned out my frustration. Those men were not mine, and never would be.

They'd wanted my magic, and they had received it. Their parents were back to being human and they could finally resume the life they'd always wanted.

I'd probably never see them again. And I couldn't even begin to explain how sad that idea made me.

It took us a week to settle our parents into the house that had once been ours but was now theirs. At first, they didn't want to see anyone outside of Leo and myself. They'd been too ashamed of how long they'd been gone and how thin and frail they were compared to everyone else in the pack.

But every day that went by brought them more strength and confidence and eventually they seemed more ready to get back out into the world. Back to the pack they'd been born into.

Leo and I had settled on the new project house, and were set to move in. We tried not to leave our parents at home alone, so we took alternating shifts at work, trying to juggle everything.

It wasn't easy, but we made it work. Just. I opened the front door and ran a hand through my hair. I'd just swapped out with Leo at the apartment we were gutting, and it was time for me to have a break.

"When are you going to see Tania again?" Mom asked from where she stood at the kitchen counter, cutting up some vegetables as she made dinner.

I slid onto one of the stools and sighed, exhaustion from the day settling across me. "I don't know." I missed her, with a bone-deep gnawing need.

Mom laughed. "What do you mean, you don't know? When your father and I met, and the fated mated link made itself known, we couldn't keep our hands off each other."

Dad had filled Mom in on all the particulars very quickly, and happily, they'd been very supportive of the double up fated mate bond.

"Tania hasn't exactly been jumping up and down to date either one of us," I told her. "Quite the opposite in fact."

The only time I'd tried to kiss her, she'd practically recoiled in horror. Looking back, I was surprised she hadn't slapped me.

Mom came over and placed her hand on mine. "Mason. I know that you haven't had an easy time. The last fifteen years have been torture for all of us. We felt so... helpless. We truly despaired and would have ended our lives if it wasn't for you boys. You were our hope. You were our saving grace."

Mom stopped to wipe away the tears that spilled onto her cheeks.

"It's okay." I patted her hand, "You don't need to say anything else."

"It's not okay. It has to be said." She stopped to take a breath, then continued. "Mason, I know you both killed yourselves working, to make money to bring us home. I know that you've both barely stopped. You've never had a long-term relationship, and you've never been on a vacation, let alone left the state."

I scrubbed my free hand over my bristled chin. "We had to save you, Mom. There wasn't any time for anything else." And I would have felt guilty if I'd turned away from my mission, even for a minute.

Mom leaned over the counter and kissed my cheek.

I pulled away. "Don't. I need a shower." I was grimy and sweat encrusted from the day.

She laughed. "Sweetheart. You are a wonderful man, and I'm so proud of you. Your father and I... we both are. And we thank you, from the bottom of our hearts for saving us from our fate. But it's time for you to have a life. It's time for a family... for you to be with your mate."

She squeezed my hand once more, then tutted as she walked over to the stove. "Why don't you have some dinner and then go to that gym of hers? You have to start somewhere, and there's never a better time than the present."

She was right, of course. Mom was always right, and I'd missed her great advice over the years she'd been gone. But I was out of energy and time too. Or that's how it felt anyway. "I'm going to have a quick shower. I'll be back soon."

I trudged up the stairs and despite the lethargy in my limbs, my cock grew hard within the confines of the shower as images of Tania filled my head. Hot water beat down on my shoulders and ran down my back, my mate's face and voluptuous body the only thing in my mind.

She was so beautiful, and yet she didn't seem to think so. I wanted to make sure she knew how desired she was. Once I got her into bed, I'd lick her from the tips of her toes up to the curve of those luscious lips. And everything in between.

I wanted to make her cum so hard she passed out. I wanted to hear her scream my name in the heights of her ecstasy, her pussy squeezing my cock tight. I'd never wanted a woman the way I wanted Tania, and my mother was right. The time to pursue her had arrived.

I grabbed my cock and stroked myself while I imagined my beautiful mate. I couldn't stop the orgasm that slammed into me as I thought about Tania writhing beneath me. My seed blasted over the shower tiles, draining my energy away. I had no control, my body hungered for her so badly.

When I was finally clean again, I dressed and ate dinner quickly, before taking Mom's advice and heading over to Tania's gym.

Leo was still at the apartment, plastering, but I wanted time with Tania, to mend whatever bridges I'd damaged the other day.

The gym was still humming when I arrived. It was just after eight o'clock and the place was full. Heavy metal music was pumping, and people were grunting and straining under the weight of whatever they were lifting.

I swiped the new card they'd sent me in the mail this week and walked into the gym. The place was packed and yet my gaze was immediately drawn to the dark-haired beauty in the corner of the room.

Tania was helping a blonde woman with her technique, talking to her and pointing out things on her body to change.

She stilled as I watched her, then turned toward me as though she'd felt my eyes on her. She froze with her mouth open. Staring at me, wide-eyed.

I could feel others turning to look as I walked over to her. But I didn't care. I'd declare to the world that she was mine, if she'd let me.

"Hi," I managed, though even that one word was difficult to articulate. My wolf was too close to the surface, wanting to claim his mate.

She nodded at me, then turned to the woman she was working with. "Jaydy, this is Mason. He's one of the brothers I told you about."

The blonde dropped the bar she was working with and stood up. She was taller than Tania, and just as curvy. But my wolf didn't stir. He knew who his mate was.

"Oh hey!" She grinned broadly, making no secret that she was studying me intently. "Nice to meet you."

"Nice to meet you too." I said, though I could barely drag my gaze away from Tania.

The blonde continued as though she couldn't see how much I wanted Tania to myself. "Tania was just telling me how many new clients have approached her this week, thanks to you."

That got my attention.

I spun my gaze around to her. "Sorry... what clients?"

"Haven't you been telling people in your pack about Tania? And what she did for you?"

"Ah... Yeah, I suppose I've told a few people." I shot a look at Tania to gauge her reaction. Mom and Dad would have been explaining the whole story to anyone who'd come to visit. I'd offered to spread the word and get more clients for her, but I hadn't actually thought about what that would mean.

More wolves around my mate. Jealousy reared up at the thought and I almost let out a growl.

Jaydy continued as though she couldn't see my discomfort. "Well don't get her too many big client jobs, or she'll retire from here and we won't have anyone to train us at the gym."

Tania shoved at the woman who was obviously more friend than client, judging by their familiar manner with each other. "Don't be stupid. I'd never close the gym, and I'm happy to help people who need it. My new magic is a gift, not something I should make money on."

"Speaking of that new magic," Jaydy said with a huge smile, "I've gotta get going. New job starts tomorrow."

She nodded good-bye and sauntered off, her big ass swinging with strength and confidence.

"She's beautiful, isn't she?" Tania said suddenly, and I realized I was staring after the blonde.

I swung my gaze back to the woman who was my mate. "She's okay, I suppose. I know a few guys in my pack who would really be into her, actually. If you want me to set up an introduction?"

I said it so that Tania would be reassured that my need was only for her. But even as I said the words, a couple of brothers Leo and I grew up with popped into my mind. Travis and Dean. Wouldn't hurt to let them know there were some hot women training at the gym. That would get Tania some new memberships, too.

Tania's mouth dropped open, her luscious lips just begging to be kissed. "Oh, I thought you might want to ask her out."

I laughed. There was no other reaction that summed up my feelings so aptly. "Me? I'm taken, sorry."

Her eyes widened for a moment, then her gaze dropped so fast I almost didn't see the pain in her eyes. But I was quicker than she was in that regard.

I took a step toward her, closing the gap between us. "Tania," I whispered calmly, lifting her chin so she was once again staring up at me. "I meant by you. If you'll have me?"

She began shaking her head. "Please don't say stuff like that. It's not funny."

"Like what?" I asked, dropping my voice to a whisper and hoping she'd be able to hear me around the thumping music in the gym. "That I want you. That I need you. That I'd marry you tomorrow if you'd say yes."

This time her eyes filled with tears, and they didn't look like the happy kind.

I grabbed her before she could run away and dropped my head to whisper into her ear. "Transport us somewhere safe. Now."

She shook her head though she shivered under my growl. "No. I can't. Too many humans here."

"Then where can we go?" I whispered again, licking the outer whorl of her delicate ear to indicate exactly what I was going to do when she got us somewhere private.

"My apartment," she gulped out. "Follow me."

She twisted out of my arms and walked into the office in which we'd first spoken to her.

I closed the door behind us and watched as she hurried up the spiral staircase and out of view.

My heart was hammering in my chest and a small part of me felt guilty that I was with Tania alone, when Leo would have wanted to be here too.

But I was the one who had offended her by trying to kiss her the other day, and I was the one she seemed to have a problem with. Leo, as he always did, had already charmed Tania.

I needed to fix this. All of it.

"You coming?" she called, and this time she sounded annoyed, no longer breathless.

I raced up the staircase after her, emerging into a small living room at the top of the stairs. "You live here as well?"

She nodded, crossing her arms over her ample chest. "It was easier to be close to work in the early years when I did most of the shifts myself. And it meant I could afford to buy the building when it came up a few years ago."

I couldn't help the smile that spread across my face, or the pride that came with knowing she worked hard for the money she had. Just like we did. It was an admirable quality.

"What are you smiling at?" she asked, sounding offended.

"Oh, nothing bad," I explained. "I just like that you earn your living the normal way, rather than just magicking up some gold."

Tania shrugged. "Witches and warlocks who do that are rarely happy. And I didn't have the capability before."

"Before what?" I asked.

Tania heaved a massive sigh, then moved to the small kitchen. "It's a long story. You want a drink?"

I nodded. "Yeah. Please."

"Beer?"

Again, I nodded, and took the drink when she offered it. "Thanks."

Tania grabbed her own beer and marched over to the sofa, crashing down on the pillows and sitting up straight, looking super uncomfortable. The heat that we'd created in the gym was gone, and the only way to get it back was to physically get close to her again.

I didn't sit on the second sofa. I walked over and sat right next to her. She glanced over at me but didn't move away.

I twisted so I could look straight at her, nursing the cold beer in one hand. "Tell me why you don't believe that I want you."

She rolled her eyes like I was the dumb one. "Look, you don't have to pretend anymore. I did the spell for you. You got your parents back. I'll even do another one if you need something else."

I reached out for her long dark hair, running my hand around the edge of her beautiful, blushing face.

She shivered, her eyes closing. Then she whispered, "This isn't fair."

"What isn't?" I asked. "That I want you? Or that you want me?"

Her eyes snapped open, anger and desire mixing together to create a deep, dark fire. "Mason. Stop it."

Words were useless. I was never going to be able to explain to her how much I wanted her. She wouldn't believe me. I'd already tried.

They say actions speak louder than words...

I reached for her face, and this time she didn't try to move away. So I took advantage and pulled her closer, pressing my lips to hers.

I couldn't stop the moan of pure pleasure that ripped through me at the first touch of my mate's mouth on mine. This was the kiss I'd been waiting for my whole life.

She gasped when I groaned louder, then I shivered as pure bliss covered me. This was everything. This was right.

Did she feel it this intensely, too? I hoped so.

Her lips opened and I pressed deeper, sweeping my tongue inside her mouth, tasting her sweetness.

When she pulled back and stared up at me, her lips bruised from my kisses, I grabbed her around the waist and hauled her over me.

Her legs spread naturally as she slid over my lap and straddled me, staring down at me like she couldn't believe this was happening.

I could. I'd been dreaming of this moment since I'd met her.

"Kiss me again," I demanded. Then added, "Please?"

She dropped her head and kissed me, this time sweeter, softer. Her hands slid up to cup my face, holding me still. A growl rose in my throat. There was no other way I could reassure my mate that I wanted her, other than this. I kissed her hard, sliding my hands around her waist, pulled her harder against me. My cock throbbed beneath her, desperate to be free.

She couldn't mistake that for anything other than desire for her, surely?

I ran my hands up her body, needing to explore her curves. I cupped her luscious breasts and flicked her nipples through her tank top, growling a little when the tips hardened under her bra.

She pushed back and stared at me. "Is this really happening?"

Words seemed insufficient, so I settled for, "Yes. At long last." Then I pulled her back down for another passionate kiss.

CHAPTER
SIXTEEN
LEO

My wolf senses told me to leave work and head home. I ignored the intuitive pokes initially. We had too much work to do for me to knock off early. But after I'd hung another sheet of dry wall, my arms were literally shaking with the stress of ignoring my instincts.

"Okay. Okay. Fine." I conceded to whatever was driving me to leave the apartment.

Instead of racing straight home, I grabbed my cell phone and called Mom. It rang for ages, then she hung up on me. I chuckled and tried again, knowing that she was struggling with the new technology.

On the third try she answered. "Hello... hello! Is someone there?"

"Yeah Mom, its Leo."

"Leo! This phone..."

"I know Mom, I know. It's all good. I was just ringing to ask if Mason was home." I wasn't sure why I asked her such a question, I could have just rung my brother directly.

"No, sweetheart. I told him to go see Tania. I think he went to her gym."

My wolf senses roared to life. I glanced at my watch. It was almost nine o'clock. I needed to hustle. "Thanks Mom."

I stripped off my overalls and threw on a T-shirt and jeans. Then I jumped in my truck and planted my foot on the gas. They were together. I could feel it. And something felt... wrong.

Well, not exactly wrong, but it was the easiest way to describe the unease that was racing through my system.

I made it to the gym within minutes. The woman behind the desk was just closing down the computer and I could tell she was about to lock up for the night. "Hey! Is my brother still here?"

She glanced up and met my gaze. "Ah... I'm not sure."

"Is Tania here?" I asked. "He should be with her."

The woman glanced over her shoulder. "Tania's up in her apartment."

"Great," I said, not sure where exactly that was, but I was going to bluff my way through. "I'll go see if they're still here."

"Oh... ah..."

I jogged past her and went straight to Tania's office, letting my instincts lead the way. The moans of pleasure and soft gasps hit me first.

I clenched my jaw tight, anger and jealousy ripping through me.

Take a breath.

I closed the office door gently so I didn't alert them to my presence, then hustled back over to the reception desk where the woman had suspicion written all over her face. I forced a smile to my lips and told her, "Mason and Tania are upstairs. I think I'll join them."

She nodded slowly. "Okay. Tell Tania I've locked up."

She was clearly reluctant to leave and I grinned at the protectiveness of the woman. Sensing she was also a witch, I said, "Don't worry. Tania's magic can knock both of us on our asses. We won't hurt her."

The woman finally smiled. "Okay. Good night."

I turned back to the office and jogged over to the room, stepped in and shut the door behind me.

My heart was hammering in my chest and I paused with my foot on the first step. Maybe I should leave them alone? Let Mason have Tania to himself, at least for this first time.

The very thought had my chest tight and hurting. No. I couldn't bear that thought. I was going up.

I took the stairs two at a time but the sight before me when I reached the top step had me freezing. Tania was topless, straddling Mason on the couch.

They were kissing passionately, Mason's hands roaming over Tania's gorgeous body. And despite the kick in the gut my envy delivered, my eyes memorized every inch of Tania's beauty.

I cleared my throat to let them know I was there. Tania gasped and grabbed for her breasts, trying to cover herself, while Mason growled out his annoyance.

I walked closer, now seeing that my brother's shirt was open and Tania's lips were lush and red from kisses.

I opened my mouth to speak, then shut it again. My throat had closed up, my wolf leaping up to take control. If Tania had chosen Mason, then there was nothing to say.

I took another step closer, then another, until I was staring down into Tania's eyes.

One word was my undoing.

She whispered, "Leo." And I couldn't walk away.

I cupped her face with my hands and kissed her, hard. Branding her, loving her, wanting her.

She moaned and reached up to cup my head, threading her

fingers into my hair and holding me to her. I kissed her deep, stroking my tongue into her mouth and tasting her.

When I finally pulled back, her head dropped back and she released a sensual moan. Mason was kissing her breasts, sucking on the dark red tips.

I was hard and aching and had no idea where the bedroom was. I straightened and looked around.

Tania's hand reached out and stroked my cock through my jeans.

A groan rose up from my throat, unbidden, and I stared down at her. "Notice that, huh?"

She nodded, her eyelids at half-mast. "You... want me, too?"

"Hell yes," I ground out, cupping her face again and kissing her once more. "More than life itself. Where's the bedroom?"

She slid off Mason's lap and took my hand, but instead of dragging me there like I hoped she'd do, she simply pointed at a door that led off the kitchen area. "Through there."

"Let's go then," I said, tugging her that way. "Assuming you want both of us? I don't want to be an unwanted burden."

She leaned forward and kissed me, softly, reverently. Her answer sat there in every touch, every look.

I glanced at Mason as he stood up, his cheeks flushed with heat. "You okay if I join too?"

He nodded, shrugging out of his shirt. "Whatever Tania wants is fine by me."

I glanced at our woman. "Yes?"

She nodded, her gaze darting between us, her cheeks flushing sweetly. "If you're both sure..."

"Me?" I asked, unbuttoning my jeans and thrusting them down my legs.

I kicked out of my shoes and pulled my shirt over my head.

Naked now, I gestured down to my cock which was at full mast and throbbing hard. "This doesn't lie sweetheart. I need you."

"Me too," Mason growled.

She began walking toward the bedroom, speaking softly as if to herself. "I have the strongest feeling this is a dream, so I'm not going to question it. Not now. Why would two gorgeous shifters want someone like me?"

I took a step closer to her. "Because you're beautiful!"

She pressed a finger to my lips, silencing me. "Don't say anymore. Just let me enjoy the fantasy."

I knew she wasn't dreaming, or I sure as hell hoped we all weren't. But if she wanted to feel the actions first and hear the words afterwards, then I was happy to oblige.

I glanced at Mase, who was stripping as well. I turned to the door and prowled forward. My brother didn't seem to be angry I was here, and the fact he'd taken the opportunity to seduce her... well, I didn't blame him for that either.

Not now that it was clear she wanted us both.

When I walked through the doorway, it was into a huge master suite. The bed was a king, and the color palate royal purples and black. It suited our witch to perfection.

But she was only half naked, still wearing her black exercise pants.

I pointed to them and grinned. "You are way over dressed. Strip. Please."

She clicked her fingers and the lights dimmed, several candles lighting up her bedside tables.

I frowned at her. "I can't see you properly."

"That's the idea." She wriggled out of her leggings and trainers.

I glanced at Mason, who shook his head infinitesimally as if to say, "Don't say anything. Not yet."

Mason stalked to the bed and grabbed Tania against him, kissing her hard and kneading her luscious ass with both hands.

"Lie on the bed, hotness," I said. "And spread your legs for me."

Tania turned to face me, then nodded and crawled onto the bed. She lay on her back and opened her legs a little, but didn't move. Not an inch. Not a moan. Not a sensual little wiggle in anticipation of what was to come.

I glanced at Mason, who had the same look of determination on his face that I was sure was on mine. It was pretty obvious that Tania hadn't had a lot of good sex, that was for damn sure.

But that would change. Tonight.

I prowled over to the bed and slid over her, pressing my hard cock between her thighs, and kissing her lips. Her skin was hot and beautiful. The effect of our connection was electric and she moaned and opened for me.

Then she waited, as if she thought that would be it. Hardly. I grinned down at her expectant face, then slid down her body until I was lying between her spread thighs, my head tantalizingly close to her pussy.

"Oh... no." Tania half sat up and tried to push me away.

I didn't move, but instead asked her, "Why not?"

She narrowed her eyes at me. "Because I don't... smell nice. It's not where you should be. Please come up."

I bent my head and inhaled her sweet, delicious scent. Whoever told her those lies deserved to be shot.

"You are perfection," I whispered, before setting my mouth to her clit and taking a long, deliberate lick.

Tania fell backward, her thighs coming together, hard, locking my head in place.

I chuckled and pushed against her strong legs so I could

breathe, though there weren't many other ways I'd rather die. But I wasn't done with this life, or her, yet.

I glanced up to see Mason climb onto the bed and lay down beside her. He began kissing her lips and fondling her breasts. So, while my brother attended to the top half of our mate, I got free rein on the bottom half.

I sucked softly on her clit then pulled back to stare at her pink perfection. She was gorgeous everywhere. Then I put my head back down and flicked my tongue over her engorged bud, again and again, listening to each cry and moan and enjoying the way she bucked beneath me. When I discovered a move she seemed to really like, I repeated it until she was crying out and grabbing for my head.

When she was wet and dripping, and her pussy lips red with desire, I moved my hand up between her thighs and slid one long finger into her. Then I added a second finger, crooking it and stroking her inside.

Her back arched and she shuddered, her channel walls squeezing my fingers hard. I glanced up. Mason was sucking hard on one of her nipples, her luscious belly trembling as her orgasm built.

I put my head to her clit and suckled softly, thrusting my fingers into her pussy again and again. She gasped and arched, trying to get away, yet trying to get closer at the same time.

Mase whispered, "Come on, sweetheart, come for us. Please."

Tania's pussy opened, then clenched tight around my fingers, and then she began to cum. Her whole body shook and she moaned in the most delicious way. She squeezed my fingers, her pussy rippling around them, making my cock harden even further.

When she finally stopped shaking, I withdrew my hand and

crawled up over her once more. Mason shifted to one side to give me room.

She lifted her legs and wrapped them around my waist, drawing me in tight.

"Please," she begged, shifting her pelvis so that my cock lined up perfectly with her pussy entrance.

The head butted up against her wet silk.

"I..." I hadn't meant to fuck her so quickly. I'd wanted to draw it out, and maybe give Mason first option since I'd been the one to interrupt them.

But my body moved without my conscious permission. The feel of her hot, wet pussy drew me in like nothing I'd ever known.

I slid inside her, deeper and deeper. Tania gasped loudly, arching her back and rubbing her breasts against my chest as I thrust into heaven.

I dropped my head so I could whisper into her ear. "You feel fucking fantastic." I tried to stifle the groan that rose after my words, but failed when she squeezed tight around me.

A soft laugh bubbled up from her. "You do too... but you're very big."

I wasn't really, not for a shifter. But she was wriggling as though she was uncomfortable so I withdrew most of the way, then when she grabbed my arms and pulled on me with a protesting shake of her head, I slid back inside of her. But this time I went slowly. I moved gently, stretching every last inch of her.

"Oh, wow..." Her eyes widened, and in that moment such a rush of love overcame me that I knew I'd never want another woman again. This was it. She was definitely the one.

She grabbed my face and held me tight as I kissed her hard and deep, wanting to stamp my possession all over her.

Then I began to ride her. Faster and faster, I fucked her

gorgeous, strong body, loving the feel of her beneath me, around me. Her huge breasts and large ass in my hands. Her delicious, endless curves. She was perfection.

"Leo... I'm... ah..."

I ducked my head and sank my teeth into her shoulder, at the tender place where her neck began, just as she began to cum. She clung tight to me, sinking her nails deep into my back as her pussy milked my cock and she screamed out with her beautiful climax.

I had no way of stopping my own orgasm now. Heat raced up my spine and down my legs, the pleasure centering at the head of my cock.

I came hard as I buried myself balls deep inside her gorgeous body, groaning out my release.

Tania cried out again and gripped me hard, her body responding to my orgasm in the best way with the shudders and trembles of her climax extending longer than the first time. I kissed her gently, and pressed my forehead to hers, never wanting to move.

She was... perfect. She was *mine*.

SEVENTEEN

MASON

The very idea of touching my brother in any way other than comradery or friendship, was sickening.

But sitting back and watching my mate as Leo took her, was amazing. Tania responded to him in every way, with gasps and groans and decadent sighs that sank right into my soul. Her nails dug into his back, hard enough to leave marks on his flesh. She wanted him, and he pleased her, and for some strange reason, my wolf was happy with that.

My mate was blissful and content, so why shouldn't I be? It seemed counter intuitive to what we had been taught about loyalty and monogamy, but Tania's feelings were the important thing here. Not some sort of stupid societal pressure to conform to a structure that suited others.

And my brother was a good man, despite his faults. Tania couldn't have a better mate than Leo. Except for me. At least, I hoped that's how she'd feel, when it was my turn to pleasure her. To *love* her.

The room filled with their heavy breathing and the sounds of kissing as they came down from the heights of pleasure. For a moment I considered pulling my cock from my trousers and sorting out my own pleasure, but that seemed disrespectful somehow. Also, I didn't want my brother thinking I was wanking in relation to him, so I stayed seated in the large recliner chair I'd found in the corner of the room.

Tania turned her head and stared at me. Her cheeks were flushed and a sheen of light sweat made her look healthy and very much alive.

She turned back to Leo and whispered something to him in such a low voice that even my advanced hearing couldn't pick it up.

Leo rolled off her and stood up, swaying a little on his feet. He looked exhausted, barely able to stand, but the dopey smile on his face told another story.

I didn't move, because despite my wolf leaping inside my chest to claim my mate, I wasn't sure what Tania wanted.

Could she handle me as well? Did she even want to?

Tania rolled up to a seated position, then scooted over to the edge of the bed. "Are you going to finish what you started? Or would you rather not?"

I'd been kissing Tania and loving on her breasts while Leo ate her pussy, so if she wanted me back, I'd jump at the chance. I stood up, my erect cock visible through my trousers showing her without words, that I still desired her.

Her gaze dropped to my swollen flesh, then she fell to her knees in front of me.

I didn't move, struck by how beautiful my mate was as she reached out for me and released my cock, then wrapped her hand around my shaft. I moaned, because I couldn't help it, and stepped closer.

She glanced up at me, her dark eyes filled with desire as she opened her lips and sucked me inside her mouth.

"Oh, *fuck...*" My head dropped back as I slid my hand around her skull, enjoying the luscious hair falling over my fingers, and her tongue sliding around my cock head.

I groaned and clenched my teeth, struggling with control. When she sent an especially delicious pulse along my cock with a particular move, it was too much. I pulled away and tugged her to her feet.

She looked at me with narrowed eyes, as though she didn't get why I'd stopped her. I chuckled and kissed her lips. "You were about to make me cum, and I'd much rather be inside you. If you can handle me as well, that is? Your choice. Of course."

She took a step back in the direction of the bed. "I'd rather we..." I grinned.

She obviously wasn't comfortable talking about sex, though I hoped that one day, that would change. There would be nothing hotter than our woman talking dirty, telling us exactly what she wanted, how and where.

"You'd rather I fuck you?" I asked, then grinned wider as her cheeks grew even rosier.

She nodded, so I rushed up to her big, beautiful body and clamped my arms around her. "I'd fucking love to." Then I kissed her, deep and hard, and for too long, until we were both panting. I was desperate for so much more.

"Turn around," I told her once we broke the kiss to breathe. "I want to take you from behind."

I saw the pleasure she took from my words. She didn't say anything, but simply twisted around and went down on all fours on the bed, presenting her ass for me.

"Damn, you're beautiful," I said, running my hands over the curves of her glorious behind.

She didn't move far, but her pelvis tucked under and her legs closed a little.

I frowned, though she couldn't see. "You don't believe me?"

She shook her head. "No. Because I'm *not* beautiful."

"Oh sweetheart." I groaned. "Open your legs and show me that perfect pussy. Arch your back."

I used my hands to encourage her to open for me once more, then moaned with appreciation when her slit came into view. "I'm sorry to tell you, but you're wrong. And this, my beautiful girl, never lies." With each word I pressed my cock to her entrance, burying the head again and again, driving us both insane judging by the way she was squirming beneath me.

She was wet and juicy, and gasped on every entrance.

"You're beautiful to me, do you hear? You're beautiful to Leo. Because you are..." I grabbed her hips and pushed my cock deep, "ours."

Tania groaned louder than I did and reached back for my hand. Her fingers spread over mine so I could hold her hand while I fucked her.

I moved slowly at first, withdrawing almost until I was completely outside, then Tania would gasp and push back and I'd feed her my cock once more.

But that carefully slow pace didn't last very long. I needed her too much and she was too responsive, too sexy, too beautiful. And she took every thrust in a way that demanded more. Demanded everything.

Over and over, I fucked her, pounding into her and giving her everything I had. And she gave just as much, squeezing me and bouncing back on my cock, showing her enthusiasm with every stroke.

Then she began to jerk, and gasp and her channel walls began to squeeze my cock. I was gone for. She began to cum and my cock exploded, pleasure shooting along the shaft and spreading through my body.

I gripped her hips and plunged deep, releasing my seed inside my mate as I threw my head back and howled. It was the most primitive noise I'd ever made in human form.

Tania screamed out, coming on me yet again, her pussy rippling around my cock and squeezing every last drop of seed from my body.

I collapsed forward and went down with her to the bed, rolling off her back so I didn't squash her. But letting her go felt wrong on a deep level, so I reached out and pulled her in close, not wanting to be apart from her for one moment.

She was breathing hard, covered in sweat and hot to the touch.

She was absolutely perfect.

"Let's get comfortable," I managed, and somehow got us under the covers and my head on the pillows, her head tucked into the crook of my shoulder.

"Leo." She called out softly, reaching her arm out for my brother.

Leo picked up the blanket and slid under the covers, pressing himself to her back and lying down beside us.

It was strangely peaceful and felt completely right for the three of us to be in the bed at once.

If this was what Fate had planned all along, then I was starting to think that she knew what she was talking about.

Tania

I'D JUST HAD sex with two men. *Two men*! Despite all the evidence to the contrary, I still couldn't quite believe it. My brain was sending me so many good hormones at one time I could barely think straight. It was like the best workout ever, coupled with alcohol, and something better.

I was still panting, spent, sweaty and absolutely blissful. I'd never known I could feel sexually satisfied, but here I was, count-less orgasms later and barely able to move.

"You were incredible," Mason said, kissing the top of my head.

I laughed and turned my face to kiss his chest, the sweetness of his skin still lingering on my tongue. "I didn't do anything. It was you two that did all the work."

And it was true. Mostly I'd just lain there and enjoyed their attentions. Talk about a pillow princess. So not my style.

Leo kissed my arm, the vibration of his laughter coursing over the hairs on my skin. "You are the best lover we've ever had. And hopefully the last one."

I frowned, my skin cooling and a strange itch making me want to get up. "Ah... can you guys excuse me for a second. I need to use the bathroom."

I didn't, but I should. Good sexual hygiene and all that. I sat up and pushed the blankets back. I was kind of trapped between two massive naked bodies. There wouldn't be a classy or easy way to get out of the middle.

"Come this way," Leo said, slipping out of the bed and flipping back the sheets.

The gorgeous blonde shifter grinned at me and my heart soared. He read my needs and wants so well. He was truly an incredible guy. Light and sunshine.

"Thanks." I slid to the edge of the bed, took a breath for courage, then stood up and raced across the room. My ass jiggled and I knew my love handles were obvious, too. The guys would be staring at my backside. They were men. Even when a woman was ugly, they'd still look. Wouldn't they?

When I reached my ensuite, I pressed both hands against the door and pushed it shut. My heart was beating too fast again, and not for the right reasons. I didn't want them telling me lies to make me feel better.

Leo was saying things that were just not true, and I expected better from him. I used the toilet then had a quick shower. I hadn't even thought about birth control. Not real, or magical, and it was too late now. I was close to my period so I should be safe pregnancy-wise... *I think...* I'd check my dates when I got to my phone.

From what I remembered from school, shifters didn't carry diseases, so I was safe there. Thought I'd do another quick read again tomorrow.

I washed away the sweat and other bodily fluids the best I could, then dried myself and put on a white toweling robe I kept in the bathroom but never used.

Thank goodness.

I glanced in the mirror, then after seeing my red face I did something I normally never did. I used magic to dry my hair and put on a layer of makeup that gave me just enough confidence to be able to walk back into my bedroom.

I was going to have to deal with Leo and Mason. We'd had our fun, but surely they'd want to leave now?

My chest ached and I realized I was holding my breath. I forced myself to breathe properly, then reached for the door handle and walked back into the room.

I only got one step before I stopped short.

The guys were both lounging on top of the covers, chatting about work... I think. I didn't really tune into their words. Their bodies were magnificent. There was no other word for them. The definition in their legs... their chest...fuck, their arms! Wow!

I'd grown up around an NFL player and I owned a gym. I looked at beautiful, functional, strong bodies every day. And yet Mason and Leo took my breath away.

Leo sat up and gestured to me with one hand. "You coming back?"

I wanted to. God, did I want to. But the very idea that these guys were pretending that I meant more to them was ludicrous. I just couldn't wrap my head around it.

Just go with it. Enjoy it while you can.

I gulped and pulled my robe around my body. Nope. My heart was in serious trouble when it came to these guys. I wasn't going to be able to just have some fun, then run.

I was already devastated that I was going to have to walk away. How would I feel in another night, another week, another month?

No. I had to end it now, before it was too late for me. And my heart.

EIGHTEEN

"Ah, probably not a good idea. I assume you guys have to get home?" They'd want to leave, right? Most of the guys I knew said there was nothing worse than waking up next to a one-night stand. They'd chew their own arm off rather than risk waking them up.

Leo frowned and glanced over at Mason. The older brother stood up and walked over to me, his cock swinging against his thighs and making my mouth water.

He reached out for me. "Tania, what's this about? I thought we'd made our intentions clear."

I pressed my lips together and shook my head. "No. You haven't."

Leo called out from the bed. "I think we need to tell her."

"Tell me what?" I knew there was something else they wanted! "If there was another spell you needed from me, you only had to ask."

Not give me the best night of my life, then take it all away.

I magicked up a chair at the end of the bed and sat on it,

inviting Mason with a gesture to sit back on the bed. The man was too distracting when he was standing.

Leo chuckled. "Oh no. Nothing like that."

"Then what is it?" I crossed my legs and pulled the robe tight around my body. I ached in places I hadn't known could ache. Deep down below my belly button, I hurt from too many orgasms. Was that even a thing?

Mason cleared his throat roughly, looking uncomfortable. "I'm not sure how much you know about shifters…"

He paused so I assumed that was an invitation to speak. "Not much, actually."

"Well, in our community, you can marry anyone you want. Of course. It's usually recommended you marry another shifter, and most people do."

I nodded. "Same in the magical community." And we all pretty much did. I knew a couple who had married non-magical humans, but I didn't know any witch or warlock who'd married someone from the shifter world.

Leo slid forward, taking over the conversation. "Well, with shifters, we have something called a fated mate. It's the person fate designed for you. Together, you're perfect. The attraction is insane, which makes it impossible to pass that person by."

I tilted my head to the side, processing what they were saying. "You mean like a soul mate? Lust at first sight?"

Mason chuckled. "Yeah, sort of. My parents had it, and a few of our friends do as well. It's not super common. It's special… It's what both of us have been hoping for our whole lives, though I never thought I'd be so lucky as to find my fated mate."

Mason was looking at me intensely, but I was waiting for the punchline. Then it occurred to me that they probably wanted my help in finding their special 'one.'

"Oh, I see." I nodded and sat up straighter on the chair. "Well,

I don't know what sort of spell will help off the top of my head, but I'll look through some books tomorrow."

Mason and Leo stared at each other like I was insane, then looked back at me.

"You... what?" Leo shook his head.

"You want me to help you find your fated mates, don't you?" I asked, feeling like I didn't understand what was going on.

The men burst out laughing, then Mason jumped off the bed, pulled me up to my feet and into his arms. My breath caught in my throat as my hands pressed against his chest. "What are you—"

"*You're* our fated mate, Tania!" Mason shook me just a little. "Don't you understand? We've both been crazy about you since the first day we saw you."

I blinked up at him, my mind whirling with the consequences of what he was saying. "But, hang on. You're saying that fate thinks we should be together, so you two don't have any say in it?"

Because, surely, they'd never choose me if they were able to make a conscious decision about it.

Mason snorted. "Only you could put such a negative spin on something so amazing. We're meant to be, Tania. So, if you'll have us... we're yours. Forever. There will never be another woman for us now. You're it, whether you want us or not."

Leo huffed out a laugh, "Mase, chill out." He grabbed my arm and pulled me toward him. "There's no pressure. If you need time to think, or just want to start dating for a bit, we're good with that too."

Leo led me to sit on the bed next to him. I blindly followed him even though my mind whirled with thoughts. I didn't want them feeling obligated to stay with me if they didn't want to. How terrible was that?

"You guys would never choose a woman like me, so why listen to this fate thing?" It sounded utterly ridiculous.

Leo flipped back my robe to reveal one of my thighs and ran a hand up my flesh. I couldn't stop the pulse of pleasure that his touch caused inside of me.

"Who said we'd never choose you?" Leo answered. "If we weren't fated I'd probably fight Mase to have you for myself, but since he's fated too and you seem to want both of us, we figured we could make it work."

"This?" I gestured to the three of us. "Make this work? For how long?"

Mason sat in the chair I'd conjured up. "You really aren't listening, are you?" He chuckled and smiled to take the sting out of the words. "Fated mates is forever. If you'll have us."

"Forever?" I repeated because I didn't believe them. They couldn't be serious?

Leo's fingers were wandering into dangerous territory as he said, "What do you want, Tania? You let us take you to bed, so hopefully that means you want us too."

"Of course, I do!" I couldn't help but agree. But they couldn't think that was enough. "You're gorgeous, and lovely, and funny and I love how hard you've worked to save your family. That's just..."

I couldn't tell them how much I truly admired that about them. I still had to fight tears when I thought about the way Mason and Leo had held their parents tight when they were finally human again.

"Then you're in? You want to be with us as well?" Leo said, a hopeful grin lighting his face.

I couldn't grasp the idea that they wanted me at all, let alone forever. "So... you guys don't want to go home tonight?"

Leo outright laughed, and Mason grinned. I wasn't sure if I should be offended or not.

"Not unless you're coming with us," Leo said.

"You don't look convinced that we want you." Mason got to his feet where I could now see the growing erection between his legs.

His cock was literally growing before my eyes, thickening and lengthening.

He reached for my hand and pulled me to my feet. "Would you like me to show you again how much I need you?"

I let him tug my hand to his cock so I could feel the heat of his flesh once more. But my heart was struggling with how this all felt. I wasn't sure that spending more time bonding with these wolves would be good for me in the long run.

I bit my lip and said as gently as possible, "Um... I'm a little sore. Do you think we could postpone..."

Mason stepped away as quick as a flash. "Shit. Sorry. I didn't even think."

I wasn't that sore, but I needed a break to let my heart and brain catch up a bit. My body was on board with more pleasure. The rest of me was worried about what sort of future I could expect.

But the fact that he wanted me again so soon made me pause. Maybe more sex wouldn't be a bad thing? Mason was right about one thing. Their cocks didn't lie. They were truth detectors for attractiveness, in the extreme.

Mason tugged me toward the bed. "No. I was being selfish. I'm sorry. Let's get some sleep. What time do you normally get up?"

I glanced at the clock and somehow it was almost eleven p.m. "Um. I'm on early shift, so sixish."

"Perfect," Leo said, jumping under the covers again. "We get up around six too."

He pulled back the blankets and I stood by the side of my bed, gaping at him. "You want to stay the night?"

Leo grinned at me. "You're really not understanding what we're saying." He patted the bed. "Come. Sleep with us."

"Hang on.," I said, casting a spell to elongate the king bed into a super king, then added another two pillows from my stock in one of the wardrobe cupboards.

Leo glanced over to where the carpet area had shrunk. "Now that's freaking cool."

The large bed was now three pillows wide, so we could sleep relatively separately.

Happy with the space, I conjured up a black tank top and underwear to sleep in and crawled into the middle.

"Oh, that's not cool," Leo said with a pout. "That's sad is what that is."

I laughed a little at his pout, despite my nerves about the situation. "I can't sleep naked." I lay down on the cool sheets and pulled the covers up.

That wasn't exactly true. I didn't enjoy it when I had in the past because I felt too vulnerable when I was alone, and right now I couldn't imagine trying to sleep naked with them on each side of me.

Mason slid under the covers and came at me to cuddle. Leo converged too. Each of them grabbed a leg or an arm and seemed to want my head on their chest.

I laughed again as they pulled at me, fighting like kids over a toy. "You know I made the bed bigger so we could each have a pillow and not have to sleep like a pile of puppies."

"Oh." Leo pulled away, frowning. "Okay."

Mason did the same thing. Their unhappiness filled the room.

I buried my face in the pillow and turned off the lights with my magic. "Goodnight."

They stayed on their pillows, but the heat of their bodies spread through the bed, warming me. Enticing me. I almost groaned and reached out for one of them. Or both.

"Hey Tania," Leo said from the darkness.

"Yeah?"

"What did you mean about your magic not being powerful before?"

My breath hitched in my throat. Should I tell them that my power was new? That it was most likely given to me by my best friend who had died in the process, and that it was tied into my physical size and strength?

I closed my eyes, choosing not to reveal everything just yet. It was still too nebulous, and emotion-charged. Instead, I settled for a half truth. "I wasn't born with a lot of power like my mom. I've had to work at it, and recently, it's gotten stronger."

Leo rolled a little closer, sneaking a hand over my waist then curling his fingers possessively over my hip. "Well, that's great. Well done."

"Thanks," I whispered, though it felt terrible to take the compliment when I had nothing to do with it.

Yes, I trained hard and had always been into physical fitness and strength. But that didn't mean I'd earned the magic I now possessed, nor that I was comfortable with it.

"Do you want to come and see our new house tomorrow?" Mason said. "It's a total knock down job, but if you like it... it might be worth saving."

Part of me wanted to make a joke about the fact that my mom had completely renovated their town house for nothing. She'd put an insane amount of magic into that property, for no apparent reason.

But they weren't asking me for my magical help. Mason was asking something else. "Will you be living there from now on?"

Mason rolled over to face me and even in the dark I could see the angles of his handsome face. "Yeah. For a while. But if you want us to buy something closer, or bigger to live in, we can do that. Now that our parents are home, and safe, our futures are free, for anyone, or anything."

My ribs squeezed tight and my heart sung in my chest. The man was practically offering me a home, a future, and everything I'd dreamed of.

But this was so much more complicated than just 'boy meets girl' and falls in love. They wanted me to love both of them, at the same time, and I wasn't even sure that was possible.

Waking up curled around my mate was a moment I'd dreamed about for more years than I wanted to admit. But feeling Tania's warm, soft body beneath my hands and pressed against my chest was even more life-changing than I imagined it would be.

I'd been lonely, for longer than I could remember. Resisting the urge to mate and bond with women over the years had been hard. Even though I'd known my past girlfriends hadn't been my fated mate, the need for closeness had been a heavy burden.

Now, I knew what complete felt like. Contentment. Perfection.

I kept my eyes closed, not wanting to move. I just soaked in this one flawless moment in time.

Tania sighed and nestled a little closer, her fleshy ass pressing up against my semi-hard cock. Within seconds, it stirred, thickening and pressing into her backside.

A soft laugh filled the room. "Good morning," she said.

I took the opportunity and thrust against her underwear-covered ass. "It could be."

She lifted her head. "What's the time? Shit. I have to get up and open the gym. My regulars will be here soon."

It was five minutes to six, and my body was fully awake. Tania went to get up, but I grabbed her and pulled her down again. "Let me hold you for just a few more minutes. Please?"

I hated the begging tone of my voice. But as Tania relaxed back against me, I realized it was totally worth it.

I put my arm around her and kissed her neck. "I hope you like the house we're going to show you today. It's got lots of potential for a future home."

She went still, then her hands came up to grab my arm where it lay across her chest. "Mason... is this real?"

I kissed her shoulder this time, biting her softly just so she would know she wasn't dreaming. "Is what real, sweetheart? My need for you?"

I spoke softly, since my lug head brother was still snoring his head off on the other side of the mattress.

"I'm never going to understand how you could want me. Don't you want a skinny little woman?"

I chuckled and moved my elbow down so I could cup one of her large breasts. "Why would I want skinny when I can have this?"

She gasped as I toyed with her nipple. "You're a boob guy?"

"I'm a Tania guy," I whispered into her ear. "Your huge ass makes me want to bend you over and fuck you. Your strong thighs make me want to lift you against a wall and fuck you. And your breasts... Grrr... the things I want to do to those probably aren't for your innocent ears."

She shivered in my arms and I realized this was something I was going to have to do with her for a long time into the future. She needed reassurance, because it was obvious that other people, men most likely, had done some damage to her self-esteem.

I kept talking because I wanted her to know the truth. "Sweetheart, the best thing about the fated mate bond is that I know, as sure as I can know anything in this world, that you're the one for me. Your personality will fit with mine, your heart will love mine, and your body is perfect for mine."

She gasped as I continued to toy with her breasts, then she giggled a little. "And for your brother too?"

I groaned. "Yeah. Even though that idiot can sleep through anything."

She laughed louder this time. "I don't know how I'm going to do this... If I'm honest. Two men... me. I just never thought it would happen."

"Well, it *has* happened," I reassured her. "We both want you and if you'll give us a chance, we'll make you feel more treasured than you ever dreamed possible."

She nodded but didn't say anything.

"Okay," I said, squeezing her tight. "Who do I have to hunt down? Which person in your life made you feel unwanted, or undeserving of us and everything we want to give you."

She didn't react straight away, so I just waited.

Finally, she whispered, "It wasn't one person. It was everyone. Kids at school, ex-boyfriends, even women who wanted to join my gym. There's a change slowly happening in the community. A respect for strength, but most men just want skinny. I'm never going to be that. I don't want to be. I like my curves."

I groaned. "I love your curves. In fact, if you just lean forward a little, I'll slide my cock right between these curvy ass cheeks..."

She squealed as I pushed her back, and scrambled out of the covers, waking Leo in the process. "I have to open the gym."

She grabbed some clothes out of the drawers beside the bed

and began tugging on sportswear including black leggings and a tank top.

Leo groaned and stretched loudly. "Good morning, beautiful. Damn, I slept well. This mattress is amazing."

"It wasn't the mattress." I muttered, my balls turning blue with no release in sight.

Tania raced to the door, then turned back. "If you guys wait here for a bit, I'll come back and get you some breakfast."

I glanced at the clock. "We'll stay as long as we can."

She smiled, and the look on her face lit me up from the inside. "Okay, great." Then she ran off downstairs.

I reached for the lamp and flicked it on, turning to my brother who was still looking dopey as hell. "Did you hear any of that stuff we were talking about?"

Leo turned his head to me and flicked an eyebrow up. "You were talking?"

I huffed out a laugh. "Seriously, mate. You can sleep through anything."

Leo rolled out of bed and staggered to the bathroom. "Yeah, anything except our mate leaving the bed. It got cold the minute she left."

I rolled onto my back and nodded my head though he couldn't see it, but I agreed. There was no way I was going back to sleeping alone after feeling the difference of sleeping next to my mate.

This morning I felt settled, but strong. Ready to take on the world.

When Leo came back out, he grabbed his jeans and pulled them on. "What were you talking about?"

I groaned. It was time to get up. I rolled up too and began to dress. "Just... stuff. I was trying to reassure her that we want her, that she's beautiful. She seems to have a problem believing us."

Leo sighed and ran a hand through his hair, tugging on the short tufts. "Yeah, I don't get it. She's gorgeous."

"But not a classic thin beauty," I conceded. "I kinda get why she feels that way, but after last night, I thought the fact that we wanted her would be plain enough."

"About that..." Leo crossed his arms over his T-shirt. "You didn't call. I just happened to come here. I hope that doesn't change anything between us."

I sighed. "I probably owe you an apology there. I shouldn't have come to see her without you. I know how you feel about her. But she already likes you, whereas she seemed freaked out by me. So when Mom suggested I come bym I just wanted to spend some time with her. I wasn't expecting to get her half naked."

Leo chuckled. "The beauty of the fated mate link, huh?"

I nodded. "Yeah. No hard feelings?"

He grinned. "Course not. We're sharing a mate for the rest of our lives... we can't fight over petty shit."

Tania marched back into the room, her face hard. "Well, you don't know if you'll be sharing me for the rest of your lives. I haven't agreed to anything yet."

I grabbed her and pulled her against me, then kissed her even though she looked pissed off. "Can't blame a wolf for hoping."

She rolled her eyes, but the light came back into her face.

Then she pushed out of my arms, whacking me on the chest on her way out. "Come eat. I made food."

And boy, had she. When we walked into the small living area the table was loaded with bacon and eggs, toast and fruit, sausages and tomatoes.

"Whoa. This is amazing."

She shrugged. "This is what my dad would eat for breakfast, so I figured you guys would like the same."

Leo sat straight away. "Your dad's a rock star."

Tania sat beside him, a soft smile on her face. "Yeah. He's a good guy. He'll be by later if you guys wanna train with him again."

I sat opposite the other two and began serving myself the bacon and eggs. "We've got a huge day at the property. We're pretty behind because of the hand-holding we've had to do with Mom and Dad, but we could try."

Tania poured some orange juice for all three of us, then took a sip. "How are they settling back into the community?"

"Better than expected, actually," I answered, reaching for a banana.

We chatted and ate like we'd been together for years, then we both kissed Tania goodbye and ran out the door.

It was past seven now, so most of the trades would have started work.

"Well, that was the best breakfast I've ever had," Leo said with a moan and a rub of his belly as we walked outside.

"Hell, yes it was." I glanced up at the large gym sign hanging over my head. "And the best part is, it's only the beginning."

We jumped into our trucks and sped off to work. The guys were in full swing by the time we got to the work site.

Jimmy, our sparky, grinned as we pulled up and jumped out of our vehicles. "You two haven't been late a day I've known you. Who are they?"

I locked my truck and slid my cell phone into my pocket. "They? Who?"

"The women you're seeing. Two different trucks. Late. It can only be one thing."

I glanced at Leo, who shrugged. I took that to mean it was my choice if I told him.

Jimmy was a shifter too, married with three kids. It was smart to let him know we were off the market. He'd let the pack know and would stop anyone else going for Tania, too.

"Yeah. Leo and I found our fated mate. Same woman, actually. A witch."

Jimmy dropped his pliers in the dirt at his feet, cackled with laughter, then scooped them up again. "Not what I thought you were gonna say. But congrats. That's great. You guys got your folks back, and your woman, all in a few weeks." Jimmy whistled and shook his head as though he couldn't believe it.

I couldn't believe our luck most days, either.

"She's actually the witch who broke the curse," I said.

Jimmy's head shot up. "Tania? The power lifter gym chick?"

I narrowed my eyes at him. "Yeah. Why?"

He glanced off to the side, then met my eyes again. "Word spread pretty fast about how good she is. I think there's a few guys that have asked her for help. And I know Curt and Joe asked her out, too."

A growl rose in my throat. "Tell them to back off. She's ours."

Jimmy put both hands up in surrender. "Will do, Mase. Just thought you should know."

The sparky turned away and walked into the apartment block we were renovating.

I turned to my brother, whose eyes were flashing with the silver of his wolf. Seeing that was reassuring. We felt the same way about our mate, and knowing there were other men interested in her galled me no end.

"Don't worry," I told him, walking toward the entrance to the building. "We'll fight off anyone who even tries."

CHAPTER
TWENTY

TANIA

I was doing clean up and wiping down the lifting benches when Jessie ran over to me with a big grin on her face. "We just had another three new sign ups. Seriously, this has been our best month ever. Are you doing some sort of promo for hot guys that I don't know about?"

I glanced up and took the sheet of paper she was shoving at me. Three new sign ups. All men.

"Are they all here?" I asked.

She nodded and her face lit up with a grin. "Yep. And they all want a tour." She gestured to the men who were striding into the gym behind her.

They were all wolves, that was for sure. Huge, hulking, grinning, young wolf shifters.

"Hey, are you the owner? Tania?" The first guy spoke on behalf of the group. He had bright, sharp blue eyes and a friendly, easy-going smile.

"Yeah. That's me," I said, plastering on my professional smile. These guys were gorgeous, but I wasn't having the same reaction I did to Mason and Leo. The first day I'd seen them I'd practically melted into a puddle.

Maybe there is something to this mate thing after all.

"Can I help you?" I asked, pulling the clipboard to my chest as they looked me up and down in an assessing way. I was used to those looks. I was young to own a gym, and men liked to try and sum me up.

But the look on his face when his gaze reached my face once more, was different. He was… coming on to me. If I was reading the look correctly.

"Yes. You can." He shot me a wicked grin. "Word around the pack is that you're the best witch around. Can my friends and I chat about you helping us out?"

I narrowed my eyes. Mason and Leo better not have told everyone that I work any spell for a gym membership. That was a one-off deal for them because their cause was worthy. "Why did you join the gym already? I haven't agreed to anything."

He frowned like he was the confused one. "Mase and Leo said the gym was good, and the chicks here were big and strong. I like my women big."

The grin he gave me had me wanting to groan, but I managed to keep it in.

"Well," I began, "I'm not on the menu, if that's what you're looking for."

His eyes widened, then he did something weird. He leaned forward and inhaled.

I gaped at him. "Are you… sniffing me?"

The guy's smile was almost sheepish now. "You've already been claimed. My apologies. I didn't realize."

Now it was my turn to be embarrassed. I turned away to hide my blush. Could he seriously smell the guys on me? "How about you come into my office and we can chat about the spell you want done."

Luckily for everyone, they hadn't joined the gym as payment for the spell. They were genuinely keen to work out and be part of the community. The spell they wanted was a simple one, and once again, was for a good cause.

"Stick around and train if you want," I said to Matthius, the big guy, as we stepped out of my office after the meeting. "Otherwise, I'll meet you and your sister tomorrow."

Matthius's sister had been born with a speech impediment that caused her no end of grief. Her big brother had come to ask me for help, and I was happy to give it.

Despite their gruff looks, these wolf shifters seemed to have hearts of gold.

"We can't hang today, got stuff to do at home. But I'll be back in the morning to train." He stuck his hand out and I shook it. "Was great to meet you, Tania."

"Likewise," I said with a grin, and nodded at the two guys he'd brought with him.

They headed off and I watched them go with a new understanding of wolf shifters. Why the magical community shunned them, I didn't know.

From the guys I'd met so far, my experience showed them to be loyal, family oriented, hardworking individuals. So, what was the witches' problem with them? What was I missing?

I finished with some paperwork then went up to the apartment for a late lunch. My cell phone was filled with messages from Mason and Leo. Some friendly enough, others hot enough to make my insides curl.

I laughed to myself as I put together a few beef sandwiches and cut up a mango. How was it possible that men like that both wanted to date me? The answer was obvious, and unfortunately it came down to the fact they believed some sort of god-like-entity, Fate, had chosen me for them.

It was romantic, in a way, until the way they'd explained it made it sound almost like an arranged marriage. No choice. Just... here you go. This is your person. Go ahead and breed.

Though... fucking hell, the sex was as hot as Hades. So maybe the attraction between us wasn't forced.

And I still hadn't totally gotten my head around the fact there were two of them. What were my parents going to say?

Almost as though my thoughts had conjured them up, I heard my dad's voice boom up the stairs and into my lounge. "Can I smell roast beef?"

A giggle escaped my lips. "Yeah. You can. Want a sandwich?"

"Four please!" Dad stomped his way up the spiral staircase.

I chuckled again as I magicked up another loaf of bread and got cutting into the roast meat.

"Hey Dad," I called out as he stepped onto the landing and walked across to the kitchen to hug me. "Mom with you?"

"Nah. She had a catch up this afternoon with some school friends. Just me."

"Here you go." I pushed the plate at him across the kitchen counter.

I was certain my dad had eaten lunch already. Mom served him lunch at noon on the dot. The massive plate of sandwiches I'd put in front of him would simply be an afternoon snack for my father.

"So, what's going on with you?" Dad asked, biting into the first one.

I shrugged. "You know. Work, work..."

"What about those two shifters? What are their names again?"

I swallowed hard, taking a sip of my water before answering, trying to sound casual. "You mean Mason and Leo. The two guys that were here the other day?"

"Yeah, the ones your mother and you helped out. She wants to go and visit their parents again, just so you know. She's been giving them space, but you know what she's like. She wants to get up in everyone's business."

I chuckled and ate the rest of my lunch.

When I got up to clean and took the dishes to the sink, my dad coughed, clearing his throat. "You didn't answer my question."

I shoved the dishes in the dishwasher and turned around to face him. "Oh, sorry, Dad. What did I miss?"

I didn't remember him asking me a question, but I'd been wrong before.

"How are Mason and Leo... and you? How are the three of you going?"

My jaw dropped, then I slammed it shut before he noticed my shock. How did he know? "Um... what do you mean, Dad?"

"Look, I don't want to have this conversation either. But I've been told I have to ask, and I have to give you permission to love whoever you want to... and all that jazz." He ran his hand through his hair, groaning. "As if I need to tell you that. You're the strongest woman I know. You could have ten husbands and still run circles around them."

I pulled the elastic out of my ponytail to distract myself from the super awkward conversation, then lifted it again to wrap my hair into a bun on top of my hair. "I'm really not getting what you're saying, Dad."

He groaned again. "Seriously, Tania? I can smell them both in the apartment."

My face flamed with heat. "Dad!"

"Well, tell the truth then, Tania. And I won't have to point out the obvious."

I pressed my hands into the kitchen counter and leaned forward, "I'm not used to talking to you about guys, Dad. We never have before." Which made me curious. "So why now?"

Dad sighed. "Your mother had a premonition, the day she met your shifters. She said they were going to be your husbands, which of course I didn't believe at first. But they're good guys and when I walked in here and smelt their... well... them, I realized that you'd obviously progressed your relationship. So yeah. I just wanted to tell you that we support you, baby. One hundred percent."

I didn't know what to say. Mom thought Mason and Leo were meant to be my husbands? I dismissed the idea without a second thought. Mom was wrong. She had to be. What Dad had just said was ridiculous.

He shoved his hands into his pockets, looking for all the world like a sullen teenager.

I rounded the counter and gave him a hug, needing to reassure him, as much as myself, that we were okay. "Thanks, Dad."

He kissed my head and squeezed me tight. "I know you've had asshole guys before now. But these two are different."

I nodded and closed my eyes, listening to the sound of his heart beating in his chest. "I know. I just..."

"What?"

Now that I wasn't looking at him, it felt easier to say what I needed to. "There're two of them, which is weird enough. And they're shifters which, according to all the magicals, are little better than animals."

Dad hugged me tighter and I wouldn't have been able to get away, even if I wanted to. "It's not just that, is it? I know you used to wish you were like your mother. Powerful in magic, tiny in body."

I groaned and pushed against him. "Dad!"

"No." He pulled me back into the hug. "Let me say this once, okay? I know my size worked for me as a player, and as a man. But I know you've struggled your whole life to feel comfortable in your skin. You took after me, and I celebrated that, even if you didn't."

I didn't answer, the lump in my throat was too great.

He continued. "But you're beautiful, baby. You are. And these men... they look at you the way they should. With desire, and love, and awe. So don't give up on them, okay? Don't push them away. God knows I pushed enough women away thinking I didn't deserve them."

I pulled back enough so I could glare up at him. "Seriously?"

He shrugged. "I wasn't always this comfortable, or confident. Your mother changed a lot of things for me. All good. So yeah. I said what I came here to say, so I can go home with a clear conscience."

He turned away to head downstairs again and I called out. "You wanna put in a training session while you're here? I just got a new butterfly press in today."

Dad twisted back around. "How heavy can your bars go?"

I laughed as I headed toward the stairs with him. "Let's go find out."

I couldn't wait to get back to Tania's gym and apartment. The very idea that other shifters might be moving in on her had made me as antsy as a cat on a hot tin roof all day.

"You done?" I called out to Mason around four o'clock. I'd packed up my tools and sent the guys home an hour ago. They were glad to leave. I'd been a bear all day. So had my big brother.

Mase walked over, keys in hand. "Hell yes. I can't believe I'm going to say this, but fuck work. Fuck this reno."

"Yeah totally," I laughed. "Let's go fuck our mate."

My brother and I turned to the front door. "Let's take your truck," I said. "We only need one, and we'll be back here tomorrow."

It was Friday tomorrow and thank God for that. I needed a few days with our mate to settle this hunger that was clawing inside me.

We jumped in our truck and headed straight for the gym. I rang her while we drove, but her phone just went straight to voicemail.

"She's not answering. Probably working," I said, hoping that was the only reason and she wasn't dodging our calls.

Mase growled and gripped the steering wheel tighter, the leather squeaking in complaint. "If I see any shifters there harassing her..."

I laughed through the tightness in my chest. "They won't be harassing her. They'll be trying to hire her to magic them up some tricks or trying to hit on her. You know we kinda told everyone how awesome she is."

"Yeah, well, hopefully Billy gets them all sorted out."

I nodded. That had been a good move on Mason's part. Telling Billy, whose wife was a notorious gossip, that Tania was ours. It would spread through the pack like wildfire. Any women who still had designs on us would have to back down, and any guys who thought they had a chance with our mate would disappear for good.

When we got to the gym, the red-haired chick was on the front desk. She grinned at us as we walked in and swiped our cards.

"More shifters," she said, her tone hushed. "Seriously, how did you get our number? We've had a dozen of you guys sign up in the past few days."

Mason and I glanced at each other and charged into the gym. Tania was talking to a man from our pack, James. He was a total lady's man and had gotten into every available woman in our pack twice over.

Not today.

I raced over to where they were chatting and flirting, pushed Tania back out of the way and got up into James's face. "Didn't you get the memo? She's ours."

"Leo. Hey. Stop." Tania grabbed my arm, but I wouldn't move.

My jaw was locked on and my wolf was dangerously close to the surface.

James put both hands up. "Hey mate. It's all good. I know she's yours. I can smell you all over her. It's cool. She was just giving me some workout tips. The woman knows how to lift."

The red haze began to clear, and his tone and words were making sense.

I forced my arms to relax and took a step back, shaking myself to force my shifter down. "Sorry, bro."

James grinned. "No problem. I look forward to the day I feel the same way about someone."

Then he turned and walked away.

I could feel the heated anger from Tania behind me. I didn't want to turn to face her yet. But the need to fix any problem I'd caused became too great and I eventually twisted to look at her.

She was glorious in her anger. Steam was practically rising from her ears.

"You two. Upstairs. Now." She growled at us then stormed off.

I glanced at Mason, contrite. "Sorry. Looks like I got both of us in trouble."

Mason laughed. "If you hadn't taken James on, I would have. You probably saved him a black eye."

I couldn't help but grin at the picture Mason's words roused. He was bigger, stronger, older and more aggressive than me. He was probably right. James owed me.

Mason headed off, following in Tania's wake, and I glanced over to where Jack was standing by a bench press.

I lifted my hand to wave at him, and he gestured I should come over. Tania wanted me upstairs, so I jogged over to her dad with a grin on my face. "I think I just pissed off your daughter, Jack. So I better go apologize."

Jack reached out a hand and I shook it.

"Do what you've gotta do," he said. "Sue and I were hoping to have your family over for dinner soon. Tomorrow night?"

I stared up at him, the light of recognition dawning in my brain. "Oh... yeah. Thank you. I'll just check with Tania."

Jack chuckled. "That's the right answer."

I couldn't help but laugh properly now. "Yeah. I guess it is. Hopefully I'll see you tomorrow then."

Jack nodded and dropped his arm. "I'd get going."

He didn't need to tell me twice. I raced to Tania's office, shut the door behind me and jogged up the stairs. "Sorry, your dad wanted to talk for a sec."

Upstairs, Tania was huffing and puffing as she paced the floor.

"What's going on?" I asked, because Mason didn't seem to be placating her in any way.

"You two need to stop acting like you own me. You don't!" She practically shouted the words at me.

My jaw dropped. "Of course, we don't own you."

"Then why do you keep strolling in here, declaring to the world that I'm yours. I'm not."

"But we want you to be," Mason said from his place behind the sofa. "We couldn't have made our intentions any clearer."

"But you don't even know me!" she cried. "You can't seriously think you want me."

I tilted my head. There was something weird going on here. "Tania, we know you're not a shifter, so you don't trust the fated mate link the way we do, but we're in no rush here. Date us for months, years. I know we wanted you to come see that new house, but we didn't mean to push you. If you've decided not to live with us straight away, we'll understand."

She gripped the side of her head and groaned. "Stop talking like that. You know nothing about me. You can't really believe that we're going to get married and live happily ever after."

"Why not?" I demanded. "You're meant for us! We're meant for you! Why can't you believe that!"

"Because I don't trust you!" she cried. "You just want me for my magic, and you don't realize... you don't know..."

"No, it's you that doesn't know," Mason said, his voice low and dark. "We worked like slaves for ten years to save enough money to buy our parents' freedom. We didn't even know a witch like you existed. We would have happily paid for the magic... finding you was fate. A blessing. Not something for you to question our motives over. That's insane."

"I'm insane?" She gaped at him and I groaned.

"He doesn't mean you're insane." Though thinking we seriously wanted her for her magic was a little nuts. "He means we want you. So much. We have since the moment we saw you. What's it going to take for us to convince you?"

She shrugged, biting her lower lip. "Time. I guess. At the moment everything's just happened too fast and you think I'm this powerful witch..."

Mason growled this time. "We don't fucking care if you're a witch, powerful or not. We love that you got our parents back for us, but even if you hadn't we would still want you."

She was shaking her head and crossing her arms over her chest. It was obvious she didn't believe us.

My heart was banging in my chest, panic over losing our mate beginning to ache beneath my ribs.

I forced myself to stay calm. "Come on, Tania. Talk to us. What else is going through your head?"

She lifted her hands and gripped her head. "You're shifters, I'm a witch. No-one is going to accept the union. The magics hate shifters, and you guys hate us. Your pack won't accept me."

"Fuck the pack," Mason growled.

"Well... not literally." I couldn't help the smile that lifted my lips, ever the one to lighten the mood. "The only one we wanna fuck, is you, Tania."

Mason glared at me, but at least Tania smiled a little. "I know what he means, but the pack is your family. They raised you when your parents were gone..."

Mason took a step toward her. "Yeah, and they taught us that the fated mate bond is to be respected. No matter who the woman is. Human. Shifter. Witch."

I pulled over a kitchen stool and sat upon it, again trying to lighten the mood even though I was as concerned as Mason. "My brother's right," I said. "It doesn't matter what the pack says or what they do. You're our family now. Whether you accept us or not."

"What do you mean by that?" She narrowed her eyes at me.

I glanced across at Mase for guidance. I probably shouldn't have said anything.

"Leo. Answer the question."

I looked back at Tania, willing to tell her the truth about how vulnerable we were in this regard. "If you decide you don't want us, Tania, then... that's your choice."

"Why do I hear a but coming next?"

I shrugged. "I don't know."

It was her turn to move closer. "What happens if I decide to marry someone else?"

The groan of pain that came from Mase's throat made the hairs on my neck stand on end. I tried not to flinch, but Tania didn't miss a thing.

"Tell me, Leo," she demanded.

I sighed. "Then we... just... live without you." Though living wasn't the right word. If she rejected us there would be no other mate. No wife. No children.

Tania's eyes shimmered with tears. "So you really have no choice, do you? It's me… or noone?"

How did she always manage to twist everything into something bad and wrong?

"Of course, we have a choice!" Mason said. "And we want you. Please. Tania."

"Just go," she whispered as she turned around and staggered in the direction of her bedroom. "Please. Just give me a moment to think."

She'd made it to her bedroom, and before we could say anything more, she shut the door behind her.

I stared at my brother. We should give her space, and time. Just like she asked.

"We'll lock the door on our way out," I called out to her, but she didn't answer.

Then, with my heart breaking, we left.

TWENTY-TWO

I held my breath so long I was afraid I'd pass out.

But when I finally heard my men retreat, I allowed the sob to leave my chest and tears to burn my eyes.

They have no choice!

It had been bad enough when I thought they believed a lie about fate choosing me, but to know that they believed it so completely that they'd never love another woman, it broke my heart in the worst way.

"They don't even know I'm a fraud." I sobbed, throwing myself down onto my bed where the smell of my men still lingered.

The genie spell had given me power I'd never known before, and Mason and Leo thought that was me. My magic. Naturally. What would they say when they learnt the truth?

I had to tell them. I had to convince them that they were mistaken. That they were only enamored with me because I'd helped lift the curse from their parents. And that had only happened because of Harry, not me.

I sat up on the bed, rubbing my eyes and wiping away the tears. Was that the answer?

If I got rid of my magic, would they be able to see me for what I was? A plain, chubby witch who could never hold the interest of two wolf shifters. Could I reverse the gift of the genie spell?

Or maybe I needed to lift the fated mate curse? Leo and Mason deserved to love and marry. If they weren't attracted to me against their will, surely they'd choose to move on?

I slid off the bed and rushed to the bathroom so I could splash some water on my face.

I couldn't get rid of my genie gift. The backlash could be devastating. Not just for me, but for all the other big girls that I'd wished would be more powerful.

So, the only solution was to lift the fated mate curse that had its teeth in my men.

I growled, then glared at myself in the mirror. "Stop thinking they're your men. They're not."

And they never would be. Even if Mom seemed to think we were meant to be. I didn't believe her either. She just wanted me to have an extraordinary life. She didn't realize that I wasn't her. That I may never find a man who would love me, the way she'd found Dad.

I raced to my bookshelf and pulled down one book after another. There had to be a spell about fated mates, surely?

I scanned page upon page, finding nothing.

Then finally I put my hands out and called to my new magic, asking for the book that would show me the way to unhook Mason and Leo from the mate curse. A large, dusty tome flew into my arms and I staggered under the weight.

The book wasn't familiar, quite the opposite.

I sat down on the couch and opened the book on my lap,

determined to find the spell that would unhook us all from this mess.

And once I freed my men from feeling the way they did, then maybe I could find a spell to lift the heartbreak I knew would follow once I lost them.

Better now than in a year.

I used my magic once more to flick open the front page, then the pages whirled past, fanning my face as they found the perfect spell for me.

And there it was.

Unhooking a love spell.

I pressed my lips together. Was that the right one? Really? I hadn't put a spell on them, and neither had any other witch. That I knew of, anyway. Who knew how and where the fated mates idea had come from?

I grabbed the book hard, the ancient paper crinkling beneath my grip. The spell was basic enough. I wasn't sure how much power would be necessary, but I was going to try. Mason and Leo didn't deserve to be hooked to me against their will for the rest of their lives.

With tears streaming down my face, I stood up, held out my hands and began the spell.

I spoke Mason and Leo's name when the spell asked for it and I concentrated on their faces, memories of their voice and their touch filtering through me. They didn't deserve to have the burden of being married to a woman like me.

A woman they'd never choose on their own. I couldn't handle it. I would be totally besotted with them, whereas their feelings were all linked to a spell.

A spell I was about to break.

Pain tingled along my nerves, filling my arms and going straight for my head.

The spell was almost done, and yet the magic was fighting me, wanting me to stop.

I forced the words from my throat and the spell was done. I was lightheaded and couldn't open my eyes. They felt weighed down by lead.

I staggered sideways, crashing into the sofa.

I fell onto my hands and knees, pain crushing my heart as my chest squeezed like a vice. I screamed out but there was no-one to hear me.

Everything went dark.

MASON

We were still sitting in our truck, unable to drive away from the woman we both needed. Unable to leave her, despite the last words she'd said to us.

She didn't want us.

She didn't believe we wanted her.

All was lost.

Tania's scream echoed through my head.

I clasped my hands over my ears, trying to drown out the sound even as I turned to my brother and yelled, "Can you hear that?"

Leo was already jumping out of the truck and running for the front door, which we'd stupidly locked.

I grabbed the tire iron and charged for the front door in Leo's wake.

Leo put out his hand, eyeing the tire iron. "Are you sure about that?"

I raised my arm and threw the metal bar straight through the glass door. "Absolutely." Glass smashed loudly, littering the pavement at our feet with large shards.

I reached through the hole I'd made and unlocked the front door once more. "Let's go."

Tania's scream was still ringing in my ears as I ran for her office and ascended the stairs at lightning pace.

There on the floor was a nightmare come true. My mate--*our* mate—collapsed on the floor.

I rushed to kneel beside her, feeling for a pulse at the base of her throat.

"Oh my God! What happened?" Leo called out as he raced up the stairs behind me.

"I don't know," I whispered. "But she's alive."

"Should I go for help? Or should we call an ambulance?"

I checked for any signs of injury or bleeding, and couldn't find any as I ran my hands carefully over her body. "I don't know yet."

There was a book lying next to her, open and crumpled. "Maybe she was doing a spell and fainted again? Like she did after she brought Mom and Dad back?"

Leo came over to stare down at the book. "This doesn't feel the same as last time. I think we need to get help."

I put my hand to her forehead. She was cold and clammy to the touch. "You're right. I think we need to get her to her parents."

Leo squatted down next to her, brushing her hair off her face. "Should we move her? Flip her over or get her up on the couch or something?"

I didn't like seeing her laying on her belly like that, but I was afraid to do anything that might injure her. "No. I'll stay with her. Do you think you can find her parents' house?"

Leo's eyebrows drew together. "Yeah. I know exactly where they are. Tania and I were talking about their renovations the other day."

"Go," I said. "I'll stay here in case she wakes up."

Leo nodded and ran for the spiral staircase, then disappeared downstairs into the gym.

I pulled the throw rug off the couch and lay it over Tania's form. She looked so beautiful lying there, sleeping.

I ran my fingertips over her face, memorizing every line and curve. "How could you think, for even a moment, that you aren't perfect, exactly the way you are?"

I twisted around until I could lie on my belly too, turning my head to face her. I timed my breathing with hers and listened to the thump of my heart against my ribs.

We'd only just found our mate, and even though I had to share her with Leo, I couldn't imagine any other life now than one with Tania.

And surely a woman that fate had decided needed two men to love her, would be strong enough to survive whatever this was.

"Please," I whispered. "Don't leave us. Not now. Not ever."

Tania had given us our parents back. She'd opened up our future and made us think that anything was possible.

But nothing was possible if we didn't have our mate.

TWENTY-THREE

I raced down the stairs, out through the broken glass surrounding the front door and down the street. Tania's parents had bought a monster mansion a few blocks away. I'd looked at it as a reno project for us multiple times, but had never been able to justify the budget we'd need to get it up to scratch to flip.

It was dark out and night air was cold on my cheeks as I crossed over a street and kept running.

When I turned the corner, the mansion was only a hundred feet away. There on the pavement outside the house was Sue, a shawl wrapped around her shoulders.

She rushed toward me. "I felt something. What's happened to Tania?"

"She's passed out. We don't know how to wake her up."

Sue turned to face the house and yelled. "Jack!"

She lifted her hand and there were car keys in her palm.

Jack came lumbering out of the house, pulling on a large leather jacket. "Where are we off to?"

"Tania's apartment. She's passed out and not waking up."

Jack's lips thinned but other than that, he didn't show any signs of panic. I was ready to scream with frustration.

"Hold my hand," Sue demanded. "I'll portal us there."

I nodded, grabbed her hand and closed my eyes. My heart was pounding with uncertainty. I'd never been a part of a spell, or magic before. I'd only ever seen one spell, and that had been done by Tania.

A wind rushed by my face then my skin tingled with warmth, like I wasn't outside any longer.

"Leo, thank God."

My eyes popped open and we were inside Tania's apartment. I stared at Sue with awe. "That was impressive."

She gave me a brief smile before rushing over to Tania.

"What happened?" Jack demanded.

"We don't know," Mason said, getting to his feet from his place on the floor.

He looked like he'd been lying down next to Tania.

Mason brushed off his hands. "We had a fight and she kicked us out."

"Yeah, she was perfectly healthy then," I added.

"Then what happened?" Sue asked, brushing her hands over her daughter's face and hair.

I glanced at Mase. "We don't know. We locked the front door and left like she said we should. But..."

"We couldn't leave," Mason said, lifting his chin and puffing up his chest a little. "So we just sat in the car. Not speaking."

"Then we heard Tania scream," I said, turning to Jack. "It was so weird. It was like she was screaming inside the truck cabin, but she was up here."

I still couldn't work out how she'd done it, but she'd projected her voice through the gym, outside, and into our truck.

"I think she's worked a spell she shouldn't have," Sue whispered. "And it's backfired."

"Which spell?" Jack demanded.

"There's a book under the coffee table," I said, pointing to the corner of a page I could see poking out from beneath the heavy wooden table.

"Let me get it," Sue cried.

We all froze and she grimaced out a smile. "Sorry. But we can't lose the page. If I'm going to fix this, I need to know which spell she was working that caused this problem."

I took a step back, getting out of the way of Tania's tiny blonde mom.

Sue gracefully got to her knees, reached beneath the table, and pulled out one of the biggest books I'd ever seen.

"Are all your spell books that big?"

Jack shook his head. "No. Only the ancient texts."

I shivered with the inference of the words. Tania had been messing with something she shouldn't have been, that was obvious.

Sue flipped the book over and stood up, a frown etched into her face. "I don't understand."

She moved over to the couch and sat down, staring at the page. "Let me just check." She spoke softly, white light glowing from her palm.

Then she nodded. "Yes, this was the spell she was casting. But I don't understand why this would backfire so badly. In fact, I don't understand why she'd be working it at all."

I glanced at Mase, whose nostrils were flaring with anger and worry. I suspected mine were, too.

I moved closer, since I was slightly calmer. "Maybe we can help? What's the spell for?"

Sue was sitting down, as tiny as a fairy, so I sat down on the armchair nearby, not wanting to tower over her.

She glanced up. "It's a reversal spell. A love spell reversal."

It was my turn to be surprised. "Huh?"

"She was trying to reverse a love spell on who?" Mase asked, walking closer.

I scrunched up my face, thinking hard. It didn't make sense, unless... "Oh, shit."

"What?" Mase demanded.

I jumped to my feet. "It's the fated mate link. She was trying to undo it. It's the only thing that makes sense."

Mase crossed his arms over his chest, his face dark. "Why would she do that?"

"Because she thinks it's the only reason we want her. She was trying to release us so we could go and find someone else. Fucking hell..." I ran a frazzled hand through my hair.

Jack's hand gripped my arm, turning me toward him. "Explain."

I sighed and gave him, and Sue, a rundown on what we'd told Tania.

When I was finally done, Sue's eyes filled with tears. "Oh baby, you silly, silly girl."

"But the fated mates bond isn't magic!" Mase ground out between clenched teeth. "I still want her, my heart's fucking broken. I..." He stopped talking when his throat closed up.

Then he walked away to the kitchen, the farthest he could get in this tiny space.

Sue stood up and brushed her tears away. "Jack. Pick Tania up and let's put her on her bed. I need to undo this backlash somehow."

A phone began to ring, and as Jack picked up Tania, I saw her cell phone vibrating and lighting up on the carpet where she'd been.

I picked it up and I have no idea why, but something told me to answer it. Her screen said 'Jaydy' and I was pretty sure I'd met that woman at some stage.

I hit the speaker phone and said, "Ah… hello. This is Leo."

"Leo! Where's Tania? Is she okay? I had the strangest feeling…"

Sue came running back to me and grabbed the phone. "Jaydy! It's Sue. I need help. Can you come?"

There was no answer, but instead, a large, curvy blonde materialized in the living room.

"Whoa." I gaped at her. "That was awesome."

Sue stared at Jaydy. "That's some impressive magic, Jaydy. Since when could you do that?"

Jaydy shrugged. "A couple of weeks? I don't know what happened, but I got more magic overnight."

Sue frowned. "Something's gone on here that Tania hasn't been honest about, and once she's awake, we've gotta get to the bottom of it."

I didn't know what they were talking about, but I didn't ask. I was pretty sure I'd find out soon enough.

"How can I help?" Jaydy asked, grabbing an elastic from her wrist and sweeping her long hair up into a ponytail.

"Come."

Sue and Jaydy headed off to Tania's bedroom and I joined my brother in the kitchen where he was still standing.

"I don't understand all this," I said, pressing my shoulder into Mase's arm, "But we are not losing her. Not now."

"Not ever," Mase whispered.

"Do you want to go?" I asked him, not sure what Mase needed to feel better at this point. "Do you wanna run? Go get Mom and Dad?"

Mase turned to stare at me. "Do you think they could help?"

I shrugged. "No idea. They could at least give her a different perspective on the fated mates link, and how normal and natural it is for us."

Mase pressed his lips into a thin line. "I don't want to miss Tania waking up."

Jack stepped out of the bedroom. "You've got a while. It's going to take Sue a bit to find the right counter spell, then Tania's going to need to rest."

Mason stared at the man we'd hoped would be our future father-in-law. "Jack, we didn't mean to—"

"This isn't your fault," Jack said gruffly, glancing at his feet. "If anything, it's mine."

"How?" I asked. That didn't make any sense.

Jack shrugged. "Tania's always taken after me. Little magic, but large in body and strength. Personality."

"That's not your fault," I said, "And what do you mean, little magic? Tania's super powerful."

"That's new," Jack said, his lips twisting.

"We love her size, and strength, and personality," Mase said, heading for the stairs. "I wouldn't change a thing about her, except maybe the fact she doesn't seem to want us to love her. That kinda sucks."

He looked at me. "I'm going for Mom and Dad. If she wakes up before I get back, tell her I'm not far. Okay? I'll be back as soon as possible."

Mase headed down the stairs and I glanced around at the small living area. "This place is about to get pretty packed."

Jack chuckled. "Yeah, she needs a bigger space."

"We just bought a new place," I said, then gulped down the lump in my throat that rose. "We asked Tania to come see it, so she could move in with us as soon as she wanted..."

"Things are pretty serious between you then?" Jack asked.

I looked at him, meeting his gaze straight on. "We weren't lying about her being our fated mate. If she doesn't want us, then we're done, really. We won't find another wife. We never thought we'd have to share a mate, that wasn't expected, but..."

I shrugged.

Jack chuckled again. "She's more than enough for two of you. I'm not worried about that."

"Then what is it?" I asked.

Jacked sighed again. "Tania doesn't seem to believe she's loveable. And I can't work out how that happened. We've done our best, God knows we've tried, but..."

"Jack, you've done an amazing job with Tania. She's amazing. In every way. And when she wakes up, I'm going to spend the rest of my life making sure she knows it."

Jack glanced off into the bedroom beyond him, where I couldn't see what was happening. "What if she doesn't wake up?"

I frowned at him. He was a warlock. Did he know something about this spell rebound thing that I didn't know?

I lifted my chin and stared at him. "She has to. It's as simple as that."

Jack stared at me for a long time, then eventually went back into the bedroom.

My heart was as cold as ice, fear settling inside me like a disease. I refused to think about what would happen to Mase and me if Tania never woke up.

A future without her would be unbearable and I couldn't believe that fate would finally bring her to us, only to take her away.

TWENTY-FOUR

TANIA

There was only dark vastness around me, like the void of space and time. It was peaceful here, and although a part of me knew I should be scared, I wasn't.

There was no pain. No panic. No worry.

It was kind of nice, in a way.

"Tania?" A familiar voice called out to me, breaking the silence. "What are you doing here?"

I turned around and there before me was my oldest friend. "Harry."

He opened his arms and I rushed into them, hugging him tight. "It's so good to see you!"

He hugged me back, tightly. Tears sprung to my eyes. I was so happy to see Harry again.

When he pulled back, I whacked him playfully on the chest. "I can't believe we stopped hanging out over the years. I've missed you so much."

Harry was frowning at me. "What are you doing here, Tania?"

I glanced around the strange vast space we appeared to be in. "Ah... I'm not even sure where here is."

His lips thinned. "It's a resting place between life and death. As soon as you arrived, they sent me to speak to you. It isn't your time to die yet."

"I died?" I repeated, shocked.

"Not quite, but you're on the way there."

"How?"

"You tell me," Harry said with a rueful twist to his lips. "I hoped the gift I gave you before I died would keep you alive and well for a long time to come."

I frowned and tried to think about what had happened just before I was here. "I was doing a spell. I think..." I struggled to remember, then it hit me like a Mack truck. "Oh, that's right. I was trying to lift the love spell on Mason and Leo so they could continue their life without me."

I gulped on those last words, the pain of the spell coming back to settle in my chest. "I don't know what happened after that."

"What love spell did you put on them?" Harry asked.

"I didn't!" I defended. As if I would do that to anyone. "But they said I'm their fated mate and they don't have a choice about wanting me. I was trying to give them their free will back."

Harry's eyes widened, then he shook his head. "You should have done your research before casting that spell, Tania. Fated mates for shifters aren't a result of a love spell. It's fate giving them the gift of taking the guess work out of finding their perfect match. They're not wrong."

"So, what are you saying?" I asked, my heart banging inside my chest. Had I made a mistake?

Harry reached for my hands, lifted them up and squeezed hard. "I'm saying that those two men are going to want you until the end of time, and there is nothing you can do about it."

I stared into his dark eyes, my own eyes filling with hot tears once more. "But, I don't... I mean, they can't..."

"You don't believe they could love someone as beautiful, big, strong, confident and successful as you?"

I hated that he put it so beautifully, but I nodded anyway. "You know Harry, more than anyone. I'm too much. I always have been."

A tear slid down my cheek and Harry let go of one of my hands to brush it away. "You are exactly the right amount, Tania. And you always have been. It's just gonna take two men to satisfy all the love you have inside you."

What he was saying was making sense, sort of, but my heart still tugged at me. "I..."

Then I heard it, my mother's voice.

I stared down at Harry's hand on mine. His was disappearing. "I think my mom's trying to call me back."

Harry's body became strong again, for a moment. He gripped both my hands hard. "You need to go back, but listen to me, okay? I gave you that gift so you could have everything you've ever wanted. Power and strength, happiness and love. Not just for you, but for all of those around you. Don't squander that gift, my friend. Please."

He began to fade again. His face, his features, everything was fading, as was my grip on this world.

"I won't squander your gift!" I shouted out to him as I was dragged up, up and into my body once more.

"Tania!" Mom's voice was urgent as she shook me. "Come back."

Someone was chanting a spell in the background. A witch whose voice I recognized as being familiar, but couldn't work out exactly who it was.

I tried to open my eyes, but they were heavy. I forced some life back into my body by willing my consciousness back, though it hurt. Why was I hurt?

"Tania!" My mother's relief and happiness was a palpable thing when I finally opened my eyes and lifted a hand to touch the soreness of my face.

"What happened?" I asked, my voice groggy and strange. "Did someone hit me?"

Mom ran her hand over my cheek. "No, but you collapsed and hit the ground pretty hard, I'd say. You're lucky you didn't clip the end of the coffee table. Hang on, I'll just..."

Mom used a healing spell, making a warm bliss move over my skin and I sighed as the headache and pain around my eye lifted. "Thanks, Mom."

"Is she awake?" a familiar male voice asked quietly.

I pushed to shuffle up, finding myself on my bed. Leo stood in a slightly sheepish-looking manner in the doorway.

"Hi," I managed, my heart beating harder and faster at seeing one of my beautiful, sweet wolves.

He stepped into the room, my dad's large shadow looming behind him.

Dad glanced into the room, met my gaze, nodded, then disappeared again.

"We might leave you two alone for a moment," Mom said, gesturing for someone to follow her.

I glanced to the side and saw my friend. "Jaydy! I knew someone else was here loaning Mom her magic. Thank you so much for all your help."

Jaydy reached over and squeezed my hand. "Just happy to see you conscious again. I might head home to recharge, but I'll see you tomorrow. Okay?"

I nodded and watched my friend leave.

Leo sat down on the bed, smiling at me with all the love I was used to seeing in his eyes, still there.

I gulped at the lump in my throat. "Harry was right, wasn't he?"

Leo twisted his body so he could stare straight at me. "Harry? And… about what?"

My nose was tingling with heat which meant I had to sniff to stop the tears from gathering. "Um, I tried to free you and Mason from the hold I had on you. From fate making you like me, but I'm looking into your eyes and there's still that thing I saw before."

Leo shuffled closer and reached for my hand. "You mean you can see how much I adore you?"

I chuckled roughly. "Yeah. I…"

There was a clatter of footfalls on the steps then Mason burst into the room. "Is she awake… oh my God."

He fell to his knees like my dad had walloped him on the Achilles.

His shoulders were shaking and he hung his head.

Then I realized Mason and Leo's parents were here too. They had arrived just after Mason and stood in the doorway looking concerned. Leo stood up and walked over to them.

He looks back at me and smiled softly, flicked his gaze to Mason on the ground, then shut the door to give us some space.

I stared down at my beautiful, strong, rough wolf. The last one I'd ever expected to fall apart. He was the oldest brother, the less emotional of the two. Or so I'd thought.

I slid off the bed and crawled over to where Mason was still shaking. "Hey… everything's okay."

He was shaking his head and I had to hold him. I was going to cry if I didn't. I slid my arms around his shoulders and he came toward me, burying his head in the crook of my neck and holding me tightly against his huge chest.

I closed my eyes and felt a wave of love that I'd never expected to feel in my lifetime. The wave started from Mason, swelling up and crashing over me. My soul and heart met his love, and pushed my own back, creating a larger, stronger feeling.

"I'm okay," I said again, and Mason lifted his head, his eyes red with tears.

"You almost left us."

How could I have ever thought that this man was being forced to care for me? The love I saw in his eyes was undeniable.

I hadn't meant to leave them, but in a way, he was right. I whispered, "I'm so sorry." Then I reached out to kiss him.

My hand slid over his roughened jaw and drew him closer. Our lips met like a soft prayer, then turned into a ravenous kiss.

His tongue plundered my mouth and his hand gripped my body, holding me as close as possible.

How had I ever thought that what he felt for me was wrong, or fake? Being in Mason's arms now was like coming home, but to a home I'd never known before. A beautiful home I'd only dreamed of, full of comfort and love.

When the door opened, I pulled away and stared up at the group looking in at us. "Um… we'll be out in a minute."

The door shut again and I stared at Mason's gorgeous face. His eyes had changed a little and I could now see the hurt inside.

"I didn't mean to upset you. I'm sorry," I said again.

He nodded, sniffing and wiping his face. "I don't know what I would have done if you hadn't come back."

"Come back?" I repeated as we got to our feet and dusted off our knees.

He nodded. "Yeah, I lay with you on the ground while Leo went for your parents and you were gone. I couldn't feel you anymore."

I sighed and reached up to cup Mason's face once more. He

turned into my caress and my heart ached with the love I now shared with him.

"I *was* gone. I saw Harry, actually. My friend who died."

I had to tell them the truth. "I need to tell you something, but not just you and Leo. Mom and Dad as well."

Mason stepped toward the door, "I fetched our parents for you to talk to as well, to reassure you that the fated mate link isn't magic, or force, or anything like it."

"I know," I said, stepping toward him, "But it'll be nice to see them too."

I reached for the door handle and opened the door. It was time to step up and explain why I'd been acting so small and so ashamed regarding the new magic I had.

It was time to tell the truth about Harry, the genie, and the magic that I'd never had before now.

TWENTY-FIVE

Mom transported us all back to my parents' new house. Once Ariel and Max had arrived my apartment was like a tin of sardines. It had never been designed to house four wolf shifters, two witches and the largest warlock of all time.

"Would anyone like a drink or something to eat?" Mom asked as we settled in her new sitting room.

The couches were antique and exquisite, and the room itself had been painted in a gorgeous green.

"Some sandwiches would be great love," Dad responded.

He was never going to turn down food from my mother, which was handy as I was pretty sure none of the wolves were comfortable enough to ask for anything, even if they were starving.

Mom waved her hands over the large ornate coffee table in the middle of the room. Within moments the table was filled with platters of sandwiches and cakes.

"Thanks," Dad said, sliding forward to grab a couple.

Mason's dad grabbed one also, as did Leo.

I smiled at my dad in thanks for his ability to make everyone feel at ease.

"How are you feeling now, dear?" Ariel, Mason and Leo's mom, asked.

I reached out for the mug of tea my mom was handing me, knowing it was steeped in magic, probably for healing and stress. "Thanks, Mom. I'm feeling much better now, Ariel, thank you."

Ariel smiled shyly. "You're my sons' fated mate. In time I hope you'll call me Mama also. I've always wanted a daughter."

My cheeks heated with a mix of pleasure and embarrassment. "Oh, thank you Ariel, that's a really beautiful request. Thank you."

I'd never thought about calling another woman Mom, but maybe that was because I'd never thought I'd get married.

"Max and I came to try and reassure you about the fated mate bond being real, and nothing to be afraid of." Ariel tilted her head. "But looking at you now, I have the feeling that you no longer need to hear anything from me."

I grinned at the woman who could soon be my mother-in-law. "When I was unconscious, I was visited, or I visited him... I'm not sure which it was..."

"Who did you see?" Leo asked, who was sitting beside me.

"Harry."

"Harry?" Mom repeated in a shocked voice.

I nodded and stood up, still cradling my mug of tea.

Mason was perched on the edge of the sofa I had just left, and I gestured to him. "You can sit. I need to walk and talk."

He nodded and slid down onto the spot next to Leo. They both looked tense. I needed to explain who Harry was, and fast.

"Harry was like a brother to me," I explained to everyone in the room, all sitting now and watching me intently. "He was my best friend growing up, and he died a few weeks ago. In my arms. At the gym."

Ariel gasped, then lifted her hand to cover her mouth. "Oh my."

I grimaced. "Yes, it was shocking, to say the least. But there's something else that I haven't told any of you."

My dad's brows furrowed and my stomach dropped.

"What is it?" Mom asked, filling the silence.

I gripped my mug, then tried speaking, only to stop, my fear getting the better of me.

I glanced at my men.

"What's wrong?" Leo asked.

"Are you worried about what we're going to think?" Mason asked.

I nodded, pressing my lips together.

Leo chuckled. "Say what you need to say. Never be afraid of telling us anything."

"Never," Mason echoed. "No matter what it is, we'll get our head around it." He set his jaw as though I was about to say that I'd loved Harry and could never love another.

I smiled at him, feeling relieved that what I needed to tell them had nothing to do with my love for Harry.

"What are you afraid of?" Mom asked, then gave me her serious look. "Do you need me to add a truth serum to that cup of tea?"

I laughed and shook my head. "No, I can do it. Just give me a moment."

I paced up and down the gorgeous room, taking a steadying breath, then realized I had no hope without a little help from mom.

I held out my mug and groaned. "Do it."

She waved her hand, making the water shimmer with magic. Then I drank the whole cup of tea without thinking, before I lost my nerve.

Mom's magic flowed through me, relaxing my shoulders and clearing my mind. What was I worried about again?

Nothing came to mind so I decided to face my audience and tell them the truth. "Harry died because he tried to do the genie spell, and kind of failed."

My dad's gasp was the one that filled the room. "He didn't."

"He did." I turned to the confused wolves in the room and explained that turning oneself into a genie was forbidden, and also one of the hardest spells a warlock could ever conquer.

Mom wiped at the tears that ran down her face. "The spell killed him, didn't it?"

I nodded, not feeling my mother's emotions like I normally would. The magic she'd used to loosen my tongue seemed to have made me a little numb to her feelings. Almost like I was drunk. Kind of.

"Yes, it did." I turned to my wolves and explained that the man I considered my brother was gay and had never been accepted by his parents, or our community.

"You said he kind of failed," Mason said, never missing a beat. "What does that mean?"

I smiled at him, then stumbled forward to kiss him. I was enjoying the texture of his lips when Mason gently pushed me back with a pained look on his face.

"Everyone's still here," he whispered.

I staggered back with a chuckle. "What did you put in that mug, Mom?"

She grinned at me. "Whiskey, among other things."

I laughed louder this time, my legs feeling wobbly. "I knew I felt a little drunk."

"So, tell us what you've been afraid of," Leo said. "What you've said so far is sad, truly. But not what I expected."

I gulped this time. "It's... when I said he failed, sort of, I meant, he didn't fail. He had one wish to grant, and because he was dying, he gave it to me."

Dad surged to his feet. "Tania! Why didn't you tell us?"

I gaped at him. I hadn't been worried about my parents knowing, more my men. "Because... I don't know. I was a little ashamed, I think."

"What was your wish?" Leo asked gently, a stark contrast to my father's tone.

"I didn't wish anything," I declared, feeling the need to justify myself. "But Harry was my best friend growing up. He knew that all I ever wanted was more magic. Specifically... I wanted my magic and my strength to match."

My cheeks were hot with embarrassment.

My dad sat back down but his face was hard. "What does that mean?"

Mom's magic was still buzzing through me and I leaned into it, wanting to feel that relaxation once more. "It means that with his dying breath, Harry gave me my wish. That all witches, not just me, but all big girls who are strong and healthy, have magic that match their size."

"That's why you can make jewelry now," Mom said, her voice quiet and a little shocked.

I nodded. "I didn't believe it was true, to start with. But the more spells I do, the more I realize that Harry did something truly special."

I turned to my men, facing my fear head on. "I think this is part of the reason why I didn't think you should love me. I'm not the powerful witch you think I am, not naturally anyway. I would never have been able to save your parents in the past. That spell was way above my power level."

Leo grinned at me, obviously unfazed by my words. "Not anymore, beautiful. And like we've told you in the past, the fact that you were the one to lift the curse makes us admire you and your generosity of spirit, but it isn't the reason we love you. Far from it."

It was time to kiss Leo and unlike Mason, he didn't pull away or seem fussed by the fact that everyone was watching us.

When I finally pulled away, I felt more drunk than I ever had in my life. "Whoa… my head is spinning."

Leo stood up and put an arm around me. "How about we take Tania home, and catch up tomorrow. I think she's had a big enough day as it is."

Mom and Dad came over and hugged me, but I could feel their need to talk.

"Would you like me to spell you back to the apartment?" Mom asked me.

I grabbed Leo and Mason's hands, even though it wasn't necessary, and nodded. "Yes please."

In a whirl and a moment, we were back in my bedroom. Safe and exhausted, I collapsed onto the bed. "That was so intense."

I sighed heavily as I nestled my face into the soft pillow beneath my face.

Leo and Mason came to sit with me on the bed. "How are you feeling, beautiful?" Leo asked.

I turned over and smiled up at them. "Still a bit intoxicated, but so much better."

"About us?" Mason asked.

I nodded, not wanting to sit up. "Will you both stay? Sleep with me tonight."

"Hell yes." Mason stood up to strip off.

I glanced over at Leo who was getting undressed also.

I closed my eyes, focused hard, then clicked my fingers. When I opened my eyes again, I was beneath my blankets, and in my pajamas.

My men slid into the bed with me and I moved to put my head on Mason's chest.

Leo snuggled up against my ass and I giggled like a schoolgirl as I closed my eyes. "I still can't believe you both love me."

Mason growled a little, his chest rumbling. "After today, I don't know what else we can do to prove it."

I smiled again, putting my hand over Mason's heart. "Nothing at all. Now it's my turn to show you how much I adore you."

Mason kissed the top of my head and didn't say anymore.

I fell asleep quickly, nestled in the arms of the lovers I'd rejected only hours ago. It was amazing how much had changed in so little time.

But there was something nagging at the back of my mind. A look on my parents' faces that foretold problems to come. But for tonight I would simply be happy and enjoy every moment with my men, while I still could.

TWENTY-SIX

MASON

I drifted in and out of sleep, but never lost myself in the depths of true rest. There was a real fear, deep in my gut, that if allowed myself to truly fall asleep, then Tania would be gone when I awoke.

When the sun rose over the city, beams of yellow light struck our window. We hadn't bothered to pull the curtains the night before and I was grateful for the reminder that a new day was starting, and Tania was still there. Right beside me.

"Good morning," she mumbled against my chest, rolling off to stretch beside me.

"Good morning," I managed to reply, then rolled straight on top of her.

She laughed as she lifted her chin for a kiss. "Oh... it's that sort of morning, is it?"

Leo was still sound asleep, snoring his ridiculous head off.

"I'd like it to be," I said, nipping her chin with my teeth. "But you always have final say."

Tania shifted a little, so I pushed up on my hands, only to find her opening her thighs for me to settle between.

"Come back down," she invited with a grin.

I lowered myself, as I was fully naked, back between her thighs. She was hot and welcoming, and blood surged to my cock immediately.

"Can you do that magic trick?" I asked, dropping my head to kiss her cheek and whisper in her ear. "The one where you get rid of all your clothes in a flash?"

I didn't want to have to leave her body to undress her, and wanted nothing more than to love on her.

"Yes," she whispered, unmoving.

"Then do it, please." I groaned in need, thrusting against her.

I don't know what she did, wriggled her nose or nodded her head, but in the next moment she was naked beneath me.

I gasped at the shock of pleasure that pulsed over me when my skin touched hers... all over.

I had to taste her. I dropped my head to kiss her lips and went to move further down her body. I wanted her nipples hard in my mouth and her pussy juices on my tongue.

"No. Stay." She gripped my back and stopped me from descending her gorgeous body.

"But I want to lick your pussy," I whispered. "Get you ready to take my cock."

She blushed, her cheeks turning pink beneath my gaze. "I'm already wanting it. I'm so ready."

She tilted her pelvis up and I groaned as I shifted to an angle that had my cock nudging her entrance.

Tania whispered a few words, a spell I assumed, and warm heat coated her flesh.

Lube? That was definitely smart.

"Are you sure?" I asked, then gasped as she began to rock her hips on me.

I groaned again, unmoving as her hot, wet flesh tempted me. "If you keep doing that, I'm going to have to fuck you."

She looked up at me through her thick eyelashes, her smile daring me to do just that.

I pushed up on my hands once more, lined my cock up, and flexed my hips.

"Oh, yes..." Tania moaned as I dipped the head of my cock inside of her, nudging her open, stretching her entrance and building the desire for both of us.

"More," she whispered, throwing back her head and wrapping her legs around my hips.

I wasn't rushing, not with my cock as hard as rock and her body still not quite as prepared as I wanted her to be. It had to be perfect, this time. I wanted it to be the best she'd ever had.

"Please Mason. I need you." She dug her heels into me and arched her back.

Her full breasts pressed against my chest and I couldn't stop my body's reaction as I finally thrust my cock deep inside my mate.

She cried out and pulled me down, kissing me hard.

I fucked her deep, and slow, drawing out her pleasure as long as I could. With every thrust her pussy gripped me hard, squeezing tight. Pushing me right to the edge.

"Oh, Mason..." Tania began to gasp and bow and writhe on the bed beneath me. I could tell she was close and heat raced up my back. I was damn close, too.

I moved faster, fucking Tania into the mattress over and over again. Her nails dug into my arms and her pussy clamped down on my cock.

I lost any fight I had against my own battle with control and let the reins go. My orgasm roared down on me and I buried myself deep inside my mate with a muted roar. Hot pulses of my seed flowed into Tania and she shivered in my arms, moaning loudly as her own climax took her at the same time as mine.

Lights flashed behind my eyes and pure pleasure flooded my whole body.

I collapsed onto my mate, barely able to hold myself up before finally rolling to the side to release my weight from her.

She rolled with me, complaining with a soft moan. "Awww, I like your weight, please don't leave me if you can help it."

I was still inside of her, so pulled her hip a little closer to keep the connection as long as possible. "I'll remember that."

I had been worried about squashing her so I was happy to know that wasn't something to worry about in the future. I couldn't possibly move again though, not for the next ten minutes at least.

Soft snoring filled the room and Tania giggled. "I can't believe he's still asleep. I know I wasn't quiet."

"Me either." I sighed and closed my eyes, finally feeling like I could sleep and wouldn't lose my mate in the night. "I think he may have moved at one point, but..." I sort of shrugged, an amazingly sweet bliss moving over me. "Sorry... I didn't sleep a lot and I feel amazing now..."

"Sleep, my beautiful wolf," Tania whispered, her fingertips trailing over my face slowly... softly... "Sleep."

WHEN I WOKE UP AGAIN, Tania was gone from the bed, but her voice filled the air. I rolled over and stretched out my back, Leo's laughter ringing loudly.

I sat up and looked around. They sounded like they were in

the kitchen. How late was it? How long had I slept?

God, I feel better though.

Lighter. Happier.

I slipped out of bed, walked to the bathroom and quickly jumped in the shower. I stunk of stress, sweat and sex.

I scrubbed hard, and quickly, my body feeling different this morning. Was it making love to my mate, or was there something else going on? I'd have to ask Tania when I could put the strangeness into words.

Tania wandered into the bathroom just as I was getting out of the shower and reaching for a towel.

"Good morning." She grinned at me. "Again."

"Hope you don't mind," I said, gesturing at the shower. "I just felt like I needed something... something..."

My head was filling with the strangest sensation. I couldn't think, and there was no pain, but it was like I was falling down.

"I..."

"Mason, what's wrong?" Tania asked with an urgent tone, grabbing my arm.

"I..." I couldn't speak. My tongue felt tied, my throat closing up.

"Leo!" Tania called out, but my brother didn't come. Instead I heard a distant groan.

I fell toward the floor but Tania threw out her magic, stopping me from smashing my face on the tiles.

There was a loud thump and part of me knew that my brother had fallen, too, having no-one there to catch him.

"Mason! No, no, no, no, no. Leo! No! Oh my God!"

I tried to lift my head but my eyesight was giving out and Tania was fading before my eyes.

Panic hit just as she disappeared completely and I was suddenly lying on a cold, hard floor. But it wasn't white tiles beneath my naked body. Instead, dirty floorboards pressed into my knees as I staggered up to my feet.

Where the hell was I?

TWENTY-SEVEN

I rolled onto my back and sat up, grabbing my nose which I was sure was broken. "Fuck." Damn, that hurt.

I straightened my nose with a loud crack echoing in my ears and wiped at the blood gushing over my lips.

My wolf shifter genes would heal my nose in a few minutes, but meanwhile I just had to wait for the bleeding to stop.

"Leo?" Mason called out.

I jumped up and stared at my brother who was still naked and staggering to his feet. "Oh my God, what the hell happened?" I demanded, looking around.

"And where the fuck are we, is more the question," Mase said, staring around with a hard frown.

I pushed up on the wooden floor and shrugged out of my sweater. "Here."

Mason caught the sweater and pulled it over his head, then stared down at my jeans. "You still go commando?"

I shrugged. "Yeah. Sorry."

The sweater didn't cover Mason properly, but he wouldn't be

worried. Wolf shifters rarely considered nudity anything other than a natural state of being.

Tap, click. Tap, click.

The strangest sound hit my ears and I twisted around to stare at the door to the small, dirty room we were standing in.

The door opened and a little light shone in, illuminating the dust and dinge of the room.

"Who are you?" I demanded of the woman who stood in the doorway.

"And what are we doing here?" Mason said, stepping up beside me, shoulder to shoulder.

"Cover yourselves," the woman croaked at us, stepping forward so we could see her better.

She was ancient, with long white hair and gnarled features.

She gripped a walking stick, which accounted for the tapping sound I'd heard.

Tap, click, sounded in the room as she moved one step closer, and with a flick of her wrist, we were clothed, obviously to her satisfaction.

A tight black woolen sweater weighed me down, while Mason now wore a pair of slacks and shiny leather shoes.

Despite the strange, and probably dire situation, I couldn't help but smirk at him.

They were the last clothes in the world that my brother would have chosen to wear.

I tugged at my thick black sweater and cleared my throat with a cough. "Okay, so we're covered up now. What are we doing here?"

"And who the hell are you?" Mase growled.

The woman rolled her eyes and flicked her hand again.

This time we were slammed into wooden chairs that appeared

at our backs, our wrists tied down with thick leather straps to the arm rests.

Mason yanked at his bonds and the old woman lifted her stick and pointed it at his chest.

"If you try to break free, I'll chain you to the walls, wolf."

Mase stopped struggling but he was breathing hard and fast, like he was about to shift, but couldn't.

I frowned and looked inside myself for my wolf. He was there, but he was asleep and unmoving. Fear rippled through me. It was obvious this woman was a witch, and she meant us harm. But what had she done to our shifters?

As though hearing my internal thoughts, she said, "You won't be able to turn into those creatures here. I have wards on my home to stop you lot from becoming the beasts that you are."

I stared at her, something strange and almost... familiar coming to mind.

"Do we know you?" I asked, knowing the question sound ridiculous, even to my own ears.

The woman all but glared at me. "I haven't left my home in a century. Why would you know me?"

I shouldn't. But there was something about her, about this situation, that had my mind racing. My subconscious was scrolling through the archives of memory. I just knew I had some information about this situation and my brain was looking for a clue to the answer.

"I don't know... it's just..." Then it hit me.

Tania. Sue. Their conversation that day!

"You're the witch who turned our parents into wolves!"

Mason growled at her but I only stared. I should have been angrier to be face to face with our family's nemesis, but I was more relieved to have worked out the puzzle inside my own head.

"You're the ancient they were scared of upsetting by lifting the spell," I went on, figuring that the witch already had us tied to a chair. If she'd wanted to kill us, she would have done so already. Now that I had an idea of who she was, hopefully we had a chance of getting out of here alive.

The witch hobbled over to me, leaning on her walking stick and staring at me with shrewd eyes. "You're too quick by half, aren't you, boy?"

I laughed a little, sounding nervous even though I hadn't meant to. "Ah... not usually. You must have caught me on a good day."

She glanced over at Mason. "This one got the brawns, and no brains."

Mase glared at her with the heat of a thousand suns, but she wasn't fazed by him.

I tried not to snigger, but it wasn't easy. "Ah no. Mase is all heart as well."

"Hmm... let's see, shall we?" She lifted her left hand and moved her arm toward Mason.

He began to groan, fighting his restraints as his body began to vibrate.

"What are you doing?" I cried. "Don't hurt him! He's done nothing to you!"

Mase moaned, then cried out as sweat beaded on his forehead.

"Stop!" I screamed at her. "Please!"

She dropped her arm and turned back to me, seemingly unfazed. "He does have a good heart. You tell the truth."

Mase hung his head, panting hard.

I wanted to call out to him and ask if he was okay, but I didn't want her attention back on my brother. I needed to keep her focused on me.

"I do," I declared. "Ask me anything."

She narrowed her eyes and stepped closer. "How is it that my spell was broken? Who did it?"

I considered her question for a moment, and whether or not I wanted to tell her the truth. Would Tania be able to hold her own against this type of witch? Probably not. Sue had been terrified of going up against the ancient, and for good reason, it seemed.

Should I lie, or refuse her the truth? Would we die here? And if we did, would Tania then be safe?

Seemed like a good bet to me.

The witch pointed a crooked finger at me. "Lie, boy, and I'll kill your brother." She nodded at Mase, then looked back at me.

I inhaled sharply. She would, and it was obvious that she could.

I didn't have much choice, but I'd do everything I could to protect Tania.

"Our fated mate broke the curse on our parents," I answered honestly. "Her mother didn't want to help. She was afraid of you. But our mate is a good woman, a kind woman, and she couldn't handle us suffering any longer."

"Suffering?" The woman gaped at me. "It wasn't your sacred grounds that were destroyed the day those shifters came here."

I blinked at her, not sure which way to go now. Should I empathize with her situation, or defend my parents?

I decided to go with a balance of the two. "I can only imagine how offended you were, but we were barely teenagers at the time. We've lived without our parents for fifteen years now and we couldn't continue that way."

"Fifteen years," the witch repeated, her voice shocked and raspy. Maybe she hadn't realized it'd been so long?

"Yes," I confirmed, glancing across at Mason who was still resting with his head down.

But he was no longer red, or sweating, and seemed to be biding his time for the old witch to turn her back.

Don't do it Mase. She's more powerful than either of us.

"So please don't take it out on our fated mate," I begged her, still not giving the witch Tania or Sue's names. "She was only trying to help."

The witch whirled on me. "But she should never have been able to lift the spell. My magic is the most powerful magic in this country. I am an ancient. There are none stronger than me."

She lifted her chin in defiance.

I shrugged. "I'm just a wolf shifter. I don't know anything about magic."

Playing dumb had long been one of my strong suits, but I could see the witch wasn't fooled.

"You'll tell me," she said, pointing her long, crooked finger at me. "Or I'll make you."

I clenched my teeth and locked down my jaw. I wasn't telling her who Tania was, and Mase would back me up on this decision, I just knew it.

We'd die before we put our mate in harm's way.

TWENTY-EIGHT

I paced my living room, grasping for any straws of logic that I had, and came up with none.

"Fuck!" I stamped my foot. Where the hell were they?

Someone had taken my men right out from under my nose. And it had to be a witch, or a warlock. No-one else could have magically removed them from my apartment.

"Shit! I should have put up better wards."

I'd never even thought to use my magic to strengthen my own security. I was a no-one in the wizarding world. Only those with things to steal had magical wards on their homes.

No matter. I had to find them. But how? Should I do a scrying spell? Or was there a way to follow the other witch's magic to my men?

I ran downstairs and into my gym, going straight for the heaviest weights I had. I bent my knees, grabbed the huge plate at my feet, launched it up and held it above my head.

As soon as I was balanced, I did squats, pushing the blood quickly around my body, speeding up my heart and forcing my already strong body to work hard. I had to build my magic up. I needed more.

I had to find my men. Now.

Oh God. Leo... Mason... please be okay.

I threw the plate to the ground and walked over to the largest tombstone I had, hefting it off the ground with a grunt.

I pushed my arms and legs to the brink, running across the room carrying the weight, over and over again. Once I was barely able to breathe from the strain on my chest, I dropped the weightlifting equipment and staggered to a bench.

I was exhausted and seeing spots at the edges of my vision due to lack of oxygen, but my hard work had paid off. Magic was simmering in my veins, strong and sure. I waited a few moments for the blackness to recede, then hauled myself to my feet once more.

"I'm coming, don't worry." I jogged to my office, my legs screaming at me to stop torturing them, but I welcomed the pain of the exercise. It reminded me that I'd worked hard and my magic would be stronger because of it.

The moment I stepped onto the landing, I slid to the floor, my hands stretching out to the place where Leo had been before he disappeared. His warmth was still there, his energy.

I can follow him. I know I can.

I'd never read of a spell that could follow another transportation conjuring, and I didn't have time to call my mother now. I had to follow my instincts, and trust in the true strength of the genie spell and the magic it had given me.

I spoke from my heart, putting words to a spell that had never been spoken before. My whole body transformed into vapor, moving through the wood of the floor like my men had.

The feeling was strange, almost claustrophobic in a way. But I had to push my fear aside and focus on my purpose and what I'd conjured this spell to do. I closed my eyes tight as I followed the smell of my wolves. Through the air I floated and into the sky I traveled.

They'd been taken into the woods, beyond the city. So much farther than I'd assumed. But I didn't stop, or lose focus. I used every bit of the magic I had to zone in on the scent of Leo's essence. His soul.

I kept flying through the air, past the trees and to the base of the mountains. I would have gasped if I'd been in my human form, but instead I focused on being laser directed. There, ahead of me was a small cabin in the woods.

The ancient...

Then I was moving up, between grimy hardwood floors. Leo was on the ground, writhing in pain.

Mason was strapped to a chair, screaming into a gag.

I materialized as fast as I could, planting my feet and blasting the witch with all the magic I had in my soul.

She held up her stick, blocking my offense and throwing it back in my direction.

I conjured a shield and blasted her spell away, knocking over the table in the corner. The sound of crashing and splintering wood seemed to disturb the old witch and she flinched.

"Stop," she commanded, with a hand in the air. "I have questions."

I kept my hands raised and a fire spell at my beck and call. "You kidnapped my men."

The old crony held her walking stick in two hands and leaned forward on it. "I said that I have questions. Not that you may speak."

Against my better judgment, I bit my tongue because I'd had a great-grandmother when I was younger, and she had a similar manner to this woman. I had to stay calm, and she would also, but it was hard. My chest was heaving with stress and my magic bubbled beneath my skin, desperate for release.

I didn't act, though. I waited, not taking my eyes off the witch, but keeping my ears open for anything happening to Mason or Leo. They both seemed to be breathing and were close by.

The old witch conjured a chair and sat down with a groan. "Well, that was the most interesting thing that's happened here for a long time."

I didn't move, though my arms were tiring from holding them in such an active position.

The witch waved her hand at me. "You may relax, child. If you answer my questions then you will be allowed to leave."

I narrowed my eyes. "What other conditions are there?"

The witch's eyes were a pale gray and inside the iris swirled magic I'd never seen before. "That you are honest."

I lifted my chin. "I can do that, but I can't guarantee you're gonna like the answers."

The old witch actually chuckled, then coughed. "You amuse me, child. Assuming you survive this day, you must come back and visit."

It was my turn to be amused but I knew better than to be taken in by the appearance of a frail old woman. My great grand-mother had been one of the most powerful witches of her era, even to her dying day. And she had looked like she wouldn't be able to knock down a feather.

"Well?" I asked, glancing back at my men quickly and finding them both still alive. "Ask your questions."

"How did you find us?"

I relaxed my shoulders. "May I also sit down?"

The witch nodded and a chair pressed into the backs of my knees. I sat because I wanted to preserve my strength and magic, in case I needed it.

"Answer my question, child."

I looked her straight in the eye. "I turned myself into a vapor and followed the scent of Leo's soul. I travelled through the air, over the trees, and... as you saw, up between the floorboards."

The witch gaped at me. "What is this spell you speak of?"

I shrugged. "I made it up. I didn't have time to consult my mom, or the texts."

The witch's eyes glowed and I had the feeling it was with anger, not amazement. "You don't have the power to come up with such a spell."

I sighed, showing my exasperation. "I'm not lying."

"I know you're not," she snapped. "You must be the one who lifted my spell on their parents."

She nodded toward Mason and I glanced over to see my mate, kneeling on one knee beside me. He looked like a gallant knight, or a man ready to propose. But I could see the coil in his muscles. He was ready to pounce at any given moment.

I put a hand on his shoulder, willing him to relax. This witch was too powerful, and I wasn't sure I could fight her and win if I had to worry about them too.

"Yes, I did," I said simply. "My mom was meant to help me, but when she realized it was you that had put the spell on them, she was too scared to try."

The ancient's lips quirked up. "But you weren't afraid of me?"

I shrugged. "My parents didn't teach me to be afraid. And when I asked Mom if there would be consequences to me lifting the spell, she said there wouldn't be. But obviously she was wrong."

The ancient sniffed loudly. "Normally, she would be correct. Because no-one but another ancient would be able to lift my spell."

I frowned at her. "So why are we here?"

"Because I want to know how you did it!" She ground out, obviously angry that I'd managed to untie such a strong spell from the shifters. "And the magic you used today. What you are saying is impossible."

I inhaled sharply and she caught my fear.

She lifted a finger and pointed at me. "You know why this is possible."

I nodded, and swallowed hard.

"Tell me," she said.

Tears swam in my eyes. There weren't the right words to explain what Harry had done for me. For all of us. "Could I show you?"

The witch grabbed her stick with both hands, then nodded once.

I closed my eyes and used a projection spell to share my memories with the whole room. It was time my men knew the full truth about how I got my magic, too.

When I opened my eyes, there before me, playing like a movie in vivid color, was Harry's final minutes.

"It was me," he whispered. "A spell... it backfired."

Hot tears filled my eyes and leaked down my cheeks. "No Harry... I'll fix you. Come on!" I cried.

Harry reached for my arm, his wet fingers leaving sticky, bloody fingerprints on my skin. "It's okay... Tan. It's okay."

"Why didn't you go to your parents? They could have fixed you. Helped you."

He chuckled softly. "They don't deserve the last of my magic."

"What do you mean?" I asked him.

"The spell... that's killing me. It's a genie spell."

"No! You didn't..."

He groaned, his eyes closing. "You know I only ever wanted one thing."

"For your parents to accept you for who you really are," I whispered, hoisting him higher in my arms.

I shook him a little, "Harry, I would have helped you if I'd known you were struggling this much. You could have lived here with me. We could have been the odd couple all over again."

He sighed. "I should have come here earlier, Tan. But I should have done a lot of things. Now stop and listen to me. What is your greatest wish?"

"For you to live!" I cried.

"No," he whispered. "You always said that you wished your magic matched your physical strength. Do you still wish that?"

"You remember that?" I whispered, and he nodded.

I gulped. "Yes, of course I do. But not just for me. For all the big girls out there. That our strength, our power, our size... meant something more than just being... fat."

"Granted."

Harry's head fell back and I pulled his head to my chest and sobbed my heart out. "Oh Harry, I'm sorry. I'm so, so sorry. Please Harry. Come back..."

Hot tears poured down my cheeks and I wiped them away as the vision disappeared from the air as though it had never been. My nose dripped so I conjured up some tissues and blew my nose, well aware that I was now totally vulnerable to the witch.

My heart was broken all over again.

Leo came closer, sliding his hand over my leg. "Tania... I'm so sorry."

"It's okay," I managed, blowing my nose and wiping away the final tear.

I straightened my back and focused on the witch still sitting opposite us. "Does that answer your question?"

She nodded. "The genie spell is forbidden."

My stomach flipped in anxiety. "I know. And Harry paid the

price for it." Another tear escaped my right eye and I dashed it away.

Would the ancient reverse the spell? Would my men still want me if I couldn't do magic any longer?

I fixed my gaze on the witch once more. "What are you going to do?"

The ancient stood up. "Nothing. Your wish was an admirable one, and your honesty has given me the clarity I needed."

I stood up, my legs wobbling with the effort. "So, we may go?"

She nodded. "Yes."

She turned to leave the room and I looked around, noticing for the first time the dirt floor and the unkempt furniture. Despite what she'd done, I didn't want to leave her like this. "Were you serious about me coming to visit?"

She turned, her eyebrows furrowed in seeming confusion. "Perhaps."

"My mom would like to meet you," I ventured, pretty sure my mom would be both horrified and ecstatic to meet an ancient. "Would we be able to come back sometime?"

The witch held out her hand and conjured a crystal ball. "This is a portal to guide you back. Your mother and you are welcome."

I walked forward to retrieve the gift, managed a wobbly smile, then rushed back to my men who were standing and waiting for me.

"Touch the crystal and you will be transported back to your home," the witch said. "But make sure you tell those wolves to stay out of my woods."

"I will." I glanced at Mason and Leo. "Hold onto me."

The guys grabbed my arms and with a final nod at the ancient, I called on the magic of the crystal ball, and we were back home. Safe and sound.

TWENTY-NINE

MASON

I grabbed Tania in my arms and held her tight to my chest. "Holy hell, I can't believe you got us out of there alive."

She squeezed me back, so hard my back cracked. Then she whispered, "I'm so sorry... I'm so sorry."

I pulled away so I could stare down at her beautiful face, her dark eyes glistening with unshed tears. "What are you talking about? You saved us!"

"But it was my fault you were in that sort of danger."

Leo laughed beside us, reached out and dragged Tania into his arms. "What are you talking about? It was our fault that you were pulled into danger. Our parents were the ones that had the ancient spell on them. We should be apologizing to you."

She hugged Leo so tight she almost knocked him off his feet. "I'm just so glad you're both okay."

"This place is so crowded," I said, glancing around at her tiny one-bedroom apartment. "I wish you could see the new place we bought. It needs a lot of work, of course. We don't buy them any other way. But it's big."

Tania sniffed and wiped her eyes with the back of her hand. "Let's go then. I want to get out of here."

I glanced at my brother, who shrugged. "Sounds good to me. But first..."

"Yes?" Tania paused, looking at us.

"Could you put us back in our own clothing?"

Tania burst out laughing, but then waved a hand, and the strange clothing the witch had dressed us in was gone. We were back to our own shirts, jeans and boots, and I gave a sigh of relief.

We grabbed our keys and jogged down the stairs and into Tania's gym. I took her hand in mine and a thrill of happiness passed through me.

When we walked past the place where Tania's friend had died, she tugged on my hand so that we walked around the area. After witnessing her memories, I knew why.

Tania locked up the gym and we all jumped in our truck. My heart thumped a little faster as we drove the few minutes over to the large family home we'd bought. This was it. The beginning of the rest of our life.

"It doesn't need a full gut," I began to explain once we arrived and got out of the truck. "But it definitely needs a full paint job. New bathroom. New kitchen."

She grabbed hold of my hand as we stood outside, staring up at the double-story house. "It looks great. I can't wait to go inside."

Leo grabbed his keys out of his back pocket and opened the front door. "Let's do it."

"What color do you guys like?" Tania asked. "For the walls?"

"We usually go a slight off white," Leo said. "Quarter strength Casper, or something like that."

Tania walked through the front door and placed her hand on the wall. "Okay, let's do that."

As she walked slowly down the hall, trailing her fingers over the walls, a fresh coat of paint and new, uncracked drywall followed in her wake.

I glanced over at Leo, then stared in disbelief as the renovations spread. The ugly carpet beneath our feet disappeared and polished floor boards now lay in their place.

"You guys like really modern kitchens?" Tania called from the large living room.

We bolted down the hall to join her in the kitchen.

"Ah..." Leo stared at me.

Should we let her do this? We had money, and skills. Our plans had been to build her a dream home.

But what sort of assholes would we be to refuse a gift like this? "We kinda like a mix of country cottage, and modern. You know. White shaker cabinets, marble back splash, but butcher block counters. A touch of black metal and wood."

Tania nodded and continued her path through the kitchen and living room. Everywhere she touched, magic happened. The old, pink, kitchen was transformed before my very eyes. Modern stainless-steel appliances sprung up, and fresh countertops appeared.

"We can change whatever you don't like," she said, waving her hand around. "And don't worry, I know you two could have done this whole house up for us, but I'd rather us spend time together when you get home, rather than you guys working all night and through the weekend to make this place loveable."

I gaped at her. To come home and relax with our mate would be a dream come true.

She pointed her finger at the living room and large brown leather couches appeared, with throw rugs and a few cushions for decoration.

My cock throbbed inside my jeans. She was turning me on with all her magic and talking about our future together. "Let's show you the master bedroom."

I grabbed her hand and dragged her up the stairs to the largest bedroom. Once we were there, I couldn't help sliding up behind her, putting my hands around her waist and kissing her neck.

She giggled and tilted her head to give me better access. "You guys want to go back to bed already?"

Not to sleep, of course.

"Hell yes," I said, softly biting the side of her neck in a playful move. "Can you make us a bed too?"

She gasped as I moved my hands up to cup her huge breasts, loving the weight of their soft abundance in my hands.

"Ah... yes." She waved her hands and constructed a massive wooden bed, with a built-in bookshelf and side tables.

"Big enough?" She gasped as I tweaked one of her nipples with my thumb and forefinger.

I glanced at the bed that was at least the size of a Texas King, probably wider. "Yes... perfect."

Leo walked around to Tania, cupped her face and kissed her lips. I leaned forward and whispered into her ear. "Make all our clothes disappear, beautiful."

She reached a hand back to run her fingers through my hair, then the feel of her naked flesh was in my hands, against my chest. I moaned with sheer pleasure as I pressed closer, fitting my cock against her ass cheeks. "Damn, you are the sexiest woman alive."

She giggled as her head fell back on my shoulder. "You two certainly make me feel that way.

"And we always will," Leo said as he dropped to his knees in front of our mate.

She gasped as Leo licked at her core and I set about driving her crazy in other ways, kissing her lips and playing with her breasts, until she was panting and desperate for more.

THIRTY

Love and power flowed through me in alternating waves of ecstasy and hot pleasure. The magic I'd used to renovate half our new house was still there at the tips of my fingers. Pulsing, ready to create more.

But now, I didn't want to make more furniture or design our new ensuite. That would all happen in due time, later. Now, I wanted to have some fun with all this power that I'd been gifted with. I reached out for Leo and Mason's cocks, but not with my hands. With my magic.

It twisted tendrils of heat around them, exploring their balls and moving up and down their thick shafts with a delicate touch that had both of them shuddering and groaning.

Leo rested his head against my thigh. His wicked tongue that had been loving on my clit, ceased in its ministrations. "What on earth is that?" Leo gasped out, staring up at me.

Mason moaned, his hot breath on my ear.

I grinned, loving the feeling of the feminine power that came with pleasuring my men. "It's my magic."

Mason shuddered again. "I'm going to cum if you keep that up. It feels fucking fantastic!"

I laughed softly, allowing my magic one final flick around their perfect bodies before I let the tingles of my power fade away. Their twin sighs filled the room and I couldn't help but grin. "You two drive me crazy working on me at the same time. Now I have a way of returning the favor."

Or the torture, as it was in this regard.

Mason took my hand and led me to the bed. "Do you think you can take both of us at once?"

I gaped at him. "You mean..." He wanted in my... "Maybe?"

My breath caught in my throat as fear clamped down. Ass stuff hurt, right? But did it have to? I'd never done it before but, surely, I could use my magic to make it more comfortable? There had to be advantages to being a witch with two amazing men to please.

Leo slid onto the bed on his back, stroking his hard cock which lay against his belly. "Jump on top, beautiful girl."

I had a single moment to enjoy staring down at his beauty before I did exactly what he told me to. I knelt on the bed, leaned forward and kissed the head of his cock on my way up his delicious body. The taste of him was delicious, and now it was my turn to moan in pleasure.

I swung my leg over his hips and gyrated back on his cock, not even caring about what my boobs looked like, or how big my ass was. In fact, I was loving how I felt on top of my man, especially with the way he was looking at me.

With a mix of love and hunger coating his expression.

Leo's gaze flashed silver as his shifter rose up, and his grin was almost feral as he reached for me. His hands grabbed my thighs, his fingers digging into my flesh. I shifted over him so that I could line up his cock with my pussy. As soon as I felt the head nudge my entrance, I slid down on top of him, one inch at a time, moaning loudly as he filled me up.

Sparkles of white light filled my vision when I had my mate fully inside of me. I couldn't breathe, couldn't think. This was utterly beautiful.

Mason's hands on my back brought me back to reality. I had another man to please as well. Another man who wanted to please me.

I followed his gentle encouragements and bent forward, sending magic between my legs, lubing up my ass and both their cocks.

"Damn, that's nice." Mason said, sliding his thumb into my ass.

I gasped at the sensation of feeling both of them inside of me. "Wow, that's good," I whispered, rocking my hips on Leo's cock, needing more than just this. "Go on, Mason. Do it. Please."

His thumb disappeared and he pressed the thick head of his cock to my ass. There was a single moment of nerves, then they dissipated and I pushed back against him, wanting him inside of me too.

He grabbed my hips with his hand and pulled me back, pressing his cock inside my ass slowly, stretching me in a way that was new and foreign. I grimaced at the initial invasion, then cried out as a wave of pleasure crested over me.

Feeling both of my men inside me at once, finally... it was perfection. I was made for this, made for them. Fate had decreed it, and finally, I was willing to trust her.

"I won't last long," Leo gasped beneath me, his eyes squeezing shut.

"Don't wait," I groaned out, rocking and clenching around the two cocks inside me. "Just fuck me until we all blow together."

My whispered words had both men groaning and moving

within me. Mason fucked me hard and fast from behind, while Leo held on for the ride. My belly tightened and I grabbed onto Leo's biceps, staring down into his amazing eyes.

He pumped up into me, adding to the pleasure. I saw stars, lights exploding inside my head as my body fell over the edge into a huge orgasm and I went into rounds of spasms.

Mason cried out and thrust into me hard. I reached back a hand to grab hold of his arm, and his orgasm hit like a spark of lightning. Hot pulses of his seed sent me into another round of belly squeezing, screaming climax.

Leo's head was thrown back and he cried out, coming inside me as well. White light exploded around us like a call from heaven, my magic putting on a light show as we all trembled and groaned together.

Our mating was complete. Our love was bonded, linked, and the three of us were married for all time.

I fell forward onto Leo's chest, my breathing huffing out at a rapid rate. Mason gently withdrew from my behind, leaving me feeling strangely empty, until he climbed onto the bed beside us and collapsed onto his back, one arm resting over my hips.

He was panting, and when I turned my head to look at him, a huge grin split his face. A wolf joke surfaced in my head about his big teeth, but I was too exhausted and sated to say it aloud.

Instead, I said the words that filled my heart. "I love you," I whispered at Mason, reaching for his arm and pressing my fingers to his flesh.

Then I lifted my head and stared into Leo's eyes. "And I love you, too." My beautiful men.

"You are our everything," Leo said, smiling gently back at me. There was total conviction in his eyes.

Mason leaned forward and traced a gentle pattern on my

back. The caress was caring and full of love. "We will adore you forever, Tania."

Then both of them kissed me and held me and didn't let me go. This was truly the moment I knew that, somehow, I'd managed to find my happily ever after.

EPILOGUE

TANIA

~One month later~

My arms were sore, the training Dad and George had been pushing me through insane. But I was stronger than ever, and thanks to the workouts I'd been doing, so was my magic.

"Why are you still here?" Jaydy asked, rushing up to me as I put the last of my weights back on the racks.

I grinned at her as I wiped the sweat from my brow. "I've still got heaps of time."

Jaydy put her hands on her hips and glared at me. "It's eight a.m. You're meant to be getting your hair and makeup done for the ceremony."

I rolled my eyes at her. We were both witches. She knew I didn't need more than a minute to get ready. "I'm going to have a shower and get dressed."

"Nope," Jaydy said with a wicked grin. "Sorry. Your mom made me do it."

"Wha—"

Jaydy clicked her fingers and her magic threw me several blocks sideways. I was suddenly sitting on a chair in my mother's massive main bathroom.

I looked up and there was my wedding dress, hanging over the shower rail. "Mom."

Mom came rushing into the room, holding two different bunches of flowers. "Red roses or the wild flowers?"

Both bouquets were gorgeous but my gaze tugged toward the beautiful arrangement of purple and orange wild flowers.

Mom, as always, read my response without me even speaking. "You're right! I'll change the decorations around the house to match the purple. I knew you'd like those."

Then she ran off in a flurry.

I sighed, then laughed, turning to the bathroom mirror. Behind me I saw a beautiful older woman walk into the room, her hair curled and piled on top of her head. "Hey, Angie."

My mother's best friend.

"Hello beautiful," she said, lifting her magic wand—a relic from another time. "Shall we start with your hair?"

I laughed. "Let me have a shower... a real shower please. I just finished training. Then I'm all yours."

"Training?" Angie repeated, shaking her head. "I'll never understand your fascination with exercise."

I stood up and gently pushed the witch out of the bathroom. "Ten minutes, Angie. Then I promise, you can curl and fluff and powder me as much as you want."

Her grin scared me a little but I shut the door and chuckled anyway. My mother had a gaggle of interesting friends, who'd all come out of the woodwork since they found out I'd battled an ancient, and won.

And because of my new alliance, no-one had dared to say a

negative word about the fact I was marrying two wolf shifters. Not even my dad. In fact, he seemed to kinda love my guys. They were the sons he'd never had.

I scrubbed myself clean in the shower and even washed my hair, then I slipped into a fluffy white shower robe and walked out into the bedroom. "Okay Angie. I'm ready."

My mom and her witchy best friend came running at me and I was swallowed up by a storm of flowers and makeup and lace. A hilarious and amazing start to the best day of my life.

I would soon be the official mate and wife to my two men, and our life together would 'officially' begin.

Jaydy

I watched my best friend walk down the aisle in a stunning but simple white dress, a bouquet of stunning orange and purple flowers clutched in her hand, and tried hard not to let the tears of happiness for my friend fall.

I was so pleased for Tania. She deserved to be treated well.

On her arm was her father, the pair taking up the wider than normal aisle.

They were glorious, huge smiles stretching from ear to ear.

The ceremony was simple and sweet, and I listened with my heart thumping fast in my chest. Her men were beautiful, strong and so in love it was truly awesome to witness. They stood up there, next to her, chests puffed and proud.

The ceremony was conducted in Tania's parents' backyard at their new home. The house was amazing, and the reception afterward was being hosted here, too.

Soon after the ceremony finished, the bride and her grooms went to take some photographs.

I wandered over to the place where they'd set up a bar and asked for a glass of white wine.

The bartender snapped his fingers and a glass appeared.

"Thanks," I said with a smile, took the drink and turned back to stare out at the reception area. The whole backyard had been decorated with matching flowers, a white marquee tent and beautiful antique furniture.

The area looked as swanky as any hotel with the added bonus of being an intimate, special family gathering.

"Hello?" A male voice came from behind me and I turned, not sure if the man was speaking to me, but not wanting to be rude, either.

There were two men standing there, dressed in black suits for the wedding. I wasn't sure which one had spoken.

My jaw dropped as I studied them. They were staggeringly gorgeous. Sexy as sin. And they were definitely wearing their suits, not the other way around.

They were staring straight at me.

"Can I help you?" I managed to ask.

The larger, blonder, more Viking-looking guy stumbled forward with his hand out. "I... we, wanted to introduce ourselves. I'm..."

I stared at his hand and decided to be polite. "I'm Jaydy." Then I reached out and touched his skin, a frisson of electricity passing through me.

I pulled my arm back with a start, curling my fingers into my palm. "I assumed you were from the wolf shifter side of the family. But with a zap like that, you sure you aren't a warlock?"

The guys shared a strange look and I pulled my gaze away from them. My heart was thumping too loudly and my throat was thick with emotion. I wasn't sure what was wrong with me. Suddenly, I had trouble breathing and felt the need to get away.

"There's a few of Tania's cousins I meant to catch up with. I might... go."

I started to sidle away but stopped when the darker-haired guy said, "We are wolf shifters. Brothers. Pack mates of Mason and Leo. We grew up with them."

They were making me uncomfortable. Men like this didn't speak to me. I was a chubby, single, over thirty witch, without a huge amount of power. Until this past month, that is. Thanks to a sudden increase in my powers, I'd gotten a new job and life was kinda turning around.

But not enough that I could ever think that two men that looked like this would ever talk to me, unless...

I stopped trying to creep away. "Is this about a spell? I know Tania's more powerful than me, but if you need my help on something?"

"Yes!" The Viking said, a little too forcefully.

"Sorry about my brother," the other guy added. "We know this is a wedding and everything, but could we grab your number?"

"To ask for my help with a spell?" I wanted to get it straight in my head, as to exactly what they wanted.

"Yeah... or..."

"Or, what?" I asked, crossing my arms over my chest.

When both of their gazes dropped in identical timing to my breasts, I dropped my arms. Damn it. My face flushed with heat. I was wearing a formal dress, but I'd forgotten it was low-cut.

"Or, a date maybe?" The Viking asked. "Or two?"

The brothers grinned at me and I took a step back. "Look... guys, I'm flattered, but trust me, I'm not your type. I'm boring."

The men followed my lead, moving forward as I walked backwards. It was like they were, kind of, stalking me.

"We doubt that very much," dark-hair said.

Now I was starting to panic. They were serious. "Oh no... ah."

"Jaydy!"

I turned to the sound of a familiar male voice booming my name. "Jack!" I cried with relief, hugging Tania's huge father when he came up to me. "So nice to see you."

Jack turned to the wolf shifters who nodded at me. "Nice to meet you," they said, and very slowly walked away. They seemed disappointed.

"You okay?" Jack asked. "You looked like you could use some help, not that you really need it. Your magic could blast those two away in an instant."

Jack scowled at the shifters as they walked away. As a lifelong warlock, Jack had a natural dislike of any other paranormal.

I grinned up at him. "It's nice to see Tania happy, isn't it?"

Jack grunted. "Yeah, even if it is with two wolf shifters."

I laughed at his tone. "You love Mason and Leo. I've seen how you are with them."

He shrugged. "Yeah, well those two are different."

My gaze tugged toward the two wolf shifters still hovering nearby. "Yeah... I suppose there's always an exception to the rule."

Jack slung an arm around me. "Let's go find my wife. She'll be torturing the chef, I'm sure."

I let Jack pull me away from the men and I kept myself busy all night. I'd had my heart broken before, and I wasn't about to offer it up to be smashed once again.

THE END of book 1.